Dancing with Destiny

A Step in time book three

Second edition

By Stacey Broadbent

Dancing with Destiny (2nd Edition)
Published by Stacey Broadbent
Copyright © 2021 Stacey Broadbent

First published 2017
Re-release published 2018

Proofreading by Spell Bound
Cover image from Deposit Photos
Cover Design by Stacey Broadbent

ISBN: 978-0-473-58319-4 (paperback)
          978-0-473-58320-0 (MOBI)

Dance to fill your

soul...

Contents

Chapter 1

"Get out of my kitchen!" Rory yelled, shooing Damon away with a tea towel.

"Oh, baby, don't be like that," he cooed, circling his arms around her waist and planting a kiss on her neck.

Rory giggled. "Stop! You're distracting me! This needs to be perfect." She reluctantly pulled away from his grasp, huffing as she did. "What if it isn't good enough?" she asked, a frown creasing her brow.

"Are you kidding me?" Damon grabbed her by the shoulders, turning her to face him. He curled his finger under her chin and tilted her face up so she couldn't avoid his eyes. "Babe, you're the best cook I know. That culinary school is going to be lucky to have you. Don't stress so much, okay? You got this." He kissed her forehead before turning her towards the bench and smacking her bottom lightly. "Now, get back to work, woman." He grinned and darted away before she could reach him, but it'd had the desired effect. She was smiling again.

He'd never known a woman to look so hot covered in flour before, but somehow, Rory did it. Her apron was splattered with various shades of colouring from all her fondant mouldings, her hair sticking every which way, and her face dusted with flour, but damn if she wasn't still beautiful to him.

When they'd first met a year earlier, he'd fallen for her instantly. Her wild sense of humour had him hooked right from the start, the fact that she could cook almost anything she put her mind to was an added bonus.

He watched her potter about the kitchen, her petite frame almost gliding—she really was in her element. He was so proud of her for enrolling in the most prestigious culinary school in Christchurch, *Gastronomie*.

For as long as he'd known her, cooking had been her passion. She'd been working for catering companies and had the occasional shift in one of the local restaurants when they were short staffed. But what she really wanted was to own her own café come bookstore. She envisioned having scatter pillows and bean bags for people to sit and read while sampling her tasty treats. There would be poetry nights and book signings, and it would be the place for all the hipster generation to be. She even had the perfect name picked out, *Bon-appetête-à-tête*.

"I can feel you watching me," she said, carefully placing the fondant flowers around the top tier of the wedding cake she was making. Selection for entry into *Gastronomie* was one of the most challenging things she'd ever had to do. There were several stages to it; the first had been a selection of appetisers; the second, a dish using a specific ingredient that was only disclosed on the day—Rory had been given duck; and the third, a dessert.

You had to pass each stage to move on to the next, and so far, Rory had excelled. Of the 200 students who had enrolled, only 100 remained. There was one dish left to prepare. Only 40 students could go through, so in a way, this was the most important of all.

The fourth and final stage in the selection process, the students were given free reign, where they could showcase their best dishes. There were no limits to what they could do.

Rory had chosen to make a four-tier wedding cake, each tier a different flavour and theme. Damon had happily accepted the title of 'official taste-tester'. Each flavour blend she tried went past him first. Together they had come up with some winning combos. The bottom tier was a twist on the traditional fruit cake, with hints of cardamom, nutmeg, and ginger; the next, a dark chocolate mud cake with a sweet-chilli buttercream; the third layer was raspberry and white chocolate with a cinnamon swirl, and the top tier, a light vanilla sponge with a blood-orange syrup drizzled over top before a layer of buttercream and fondant was added.

Each layer was a different colour, representing different emotions. White for purity, baby blue for faith, lilac for romance and finally, pink, for love. She had spent hours forming flowers and ribbons out of fondant, and even more time painting swirls and bursts of colour with edible paints. She was nearing the end and she was exhausted. Exhilarated, but exhausted.

"Oh my God! Rory, that looks amazing!" Maddi gushed as she and Ricki joined them in the kitchen.

"You really think so?" Rory asked, wiping her hands down the front of her apron. "I thought maybe it needed something else." She motioned her hand around the middle of the cake. "Maybe something here?"

"No! Don't you dare touch it, it's perfect the way it is," Maddi scolded, taking Rory's hands and leading her out of the kitchen. She turned her back around so she could see her cake from afar. "See? It's beautiful." She hugged her friend from behind. "Now, go and sit down and I'll make you a cup of coffee. No offense, but you look like you've been dragged through a bush backwards."

"I'd pretend to be shocked by that comment if I weren't so knackered. Who knew it would be this hard to get in." She threw her hands in the air.

"Well, I think you've done an amazing job. We're all super proud of you, no matter what happens."

"Hell yeah, we are, babe." Damon scooped her up in his arms, spinning her around in circles before collapsing on the couch with her. "Maybe I could show you how proud I am of you later…" He buried his face in the crook of her neck, kissing the sensitive spot just below her ear and making her giggle.

"Ahem," Ricki cleared his throat. "There are other people in the room," he whispered behind his hand.

"Like you haven't heard it before." Damon snickered.

"Don't I know it. The walls are pretty thin, man." Ricki placed his hand on his forehead, shaking his head. "Sometimes, I can't sleep for all the noise you two make."

"Oh rubbish!" Maddi said, playfully nudging him with her elbow. "We don't hear a thing."

"Sure we don't," he said before mouthing "we do" and nodding behind her back.

"Guess we'll have to try harder then," Damon said with a grin.

Maddi rolled her eyes, chuckling. "Who else wants a coffee?" Everyone nodded their heads eagerly as she filled the jug and got some cups down from the cupboard. "You want two scoops of coffee, Rory?"

"Mmm, please. I can barely keep my eyes open. Do we have any toothpicks or match sticks or whatever it is you use to prop them open?" She yawned loudly, covering her mouth with the back of her hand.

"Why don't you go and have a rest? You've been at it for hours," Damon suggested.

"No, I'm good. I've still gotta clean up my mess and then get it down to *Gastronomie* before the deadline."

"Don't be silly, we can clean up for you. Can't we, boys?" Maddi placed her hands on her hips in a no-nonsense way.

"Of course," Ricki said.

"Ain't no way I'm getting on your bad side, Maddi." Damon pretended to look scared. "We know how good we have it here, there's no way I'm gonna jeopardise my chance of having another one of your supreme roasts, or my girl's red velvet cakes." He jumped up from the couch, pushing his sleeves up. "I'll wash, you dry," he said to Ricki.

"You got it."

Maddi set their coffees on the counter for them before carrying hers and Rory's through to the lounge. "Here ya go, hon."

Rory closed her eyes and inhaled deeply. "Mmmmmm. Coffee, how I love thee."

"And I'm sure it loves you too." Maddi grinned. "So, when do you find out if you've been selected?"

"Like, 7PM I think. We have to have it in no later than five, which gives me just over an hour to get showered and presentable." She stared off into space, her eyes glazing over.

"Hey," Maddi said, snapping her fingers to get her attention. "You're gonna be fine." She lay a reassuring hand on her knee before standing up. "Now, what are you going to wear?"

Chapter 2

"You're what?" Sacha asked, folding her arms across her chest.

"I'm moving out," Jessie said, raking his hand through his hair. "It's just not working. I can't do this anymore."

"No."

"No?"

"No. That's a lame-ass excuse and you know it. Tell me the real reason." She started tapping her toe up and down. "There's someone else, isn't there?"

"No, Sacha. I swear. There's no one else. I just…" He looked around the room as if searching for something to say.

"You just what?" she said, putting emphasis on the 'T'. He could see she was angry, not that he'd expected anything else from her. How do you tell someone you love that you feel like they're dragging you down? That they're like a poison, slowly eating away at your insides.

"I just need a break from all this…" He waved his hand between the two of them. "From us."

"Are you seriously pulling the "we need a break" bullshit? What does that even mean?"

"I don't know what you want me to say, Sacha!" Jessie wasn't normally one to raise his voice, but she could always bring that side out of him, and he hated it.

"Just say it."

"Okay, you want to know why? Because… Because I can't take it anymore." He raked a hand through his hair.

She huffed out a laugh. "I can't take it anymore," she mimicked.

"This is exactly what I'm talking about. The sarcasm, the nastiness. The constant looking over my shoulder to see if you've got your claws into someone else."

She opened her mouth to speak but he held his hand up to stop her. "Don't even try to deny it, Sacha. I'm not blind, and I'm not stupid. Or are you forgetting about that little episode with Ricki last year?"

"Ricki? What would I want with that loser?" she spat.

"Right. Of course. He's a loser because he didn't fall under your spell like I did."

"What's that supposed to mean?"

"Come on, I know you only used me. You thought you'd picked a winner, but you were wrong. You backed the wrong horse. You don't need to pretend anymore, Sacha. I can see it in your eyes when we dance. You don't love me. I don't even know if you ever did."

Sacha blinked, taken aback by his words. Her eyes narrowed and she pointed a manicured finger in his face. "You will never find anyone else like me."

"You know what? I'm actually fine with that." He picked up his bag and turned towards the door. "I'll be back to pick up my stuff tomorrow. Maybe you could be elsewhere when I do." And with that, he opened the door and walked away.

Sacha just stood there, watching, and waiting for him to come back through. This isn't how things worked. She was the one who did the leaving, not the other way around. Her hands kept balling into fists by her side, and she felt the tiniest of pinpricks behind her eyes.

No.

Crying? Over a boy? What was wrong with her? She didn't do that.

She quickly wiped her arm across her face in the hopes that it would stop the tears from falling, but it only made them fall faster.

He left.

He actually left.

And now I'm all alone.

Chapter 3

"Stop pacing."

Rory flicked her hands up and down in front of her as she treaded back and forth down the hall. "I can't, I'm too nervous."

"It's out of your hands now, just relax," Maddi said. "Come on, let's get out of the house for a bit. Why don't you come to Feeney's with us? Let your hair down."

Rory stared at her as if she were crazy. "I can't leave! They could ring any minute!"

"And you'll have your phone with you, so it's not a big deal." She turned to Damon. "A little help, please?"

He took hold of Rory's hands and led her reluctantly down the hall and into the bedroom. "We'll be ready in fifteen," he called over his shoulder.

"Fifteen? I'm gonna need at least half an hour to get ready to go out," Rory piped up from behind him. "It's like you don't even know me."

"Oh, I know you better than you think," he said with a smirk. "Don't worry, I'll have her primped and primed and ready to party in no time." He winked at Maddi then closed the door. She could hear low murmuring, followed by the unmistakeable sound of Rory giggling. She could always count on Damon to get her out of a slump.

Padding back to her own room, Maddi wondered where Ricki had got to. He'd disappeared around the same time as Rory had taken her cake down to the school, and she hadn't heard from him. She checked her watch, 6:55PM. He was cutting it fine if they were to make it to Feeney's before the crowds.

She opened her wardrobe and pulled out her favourite blue strapless dress, slinging it onto the bed along with a pair of dance tights and some silver heels. She stood in front of her mirror, tapping her chin as she contemplated how she would wear her hair.

"You will look beautiful no matter what you wear," Ricki said from behind her. He wrapped his arms around her waist and pulled her into him. "Sorry I'm so late, I lost track of time."

"You're here, that's the main thing." Maddi smiled at his reflection. "I've convinced Rory and Damon to come with us tonight too."

"Yeah? We haven't done that in a while."

"Yeah. I thought Rory could do with the distraction. She was wearing the carpet thin in the hall with all her pacing." She chuckled. "Come on, we should get organised. I wanna have that dancefloor to ourselves for a bit before all the girls come flocking to take you away."

"I think you have that around the wrong way. You're the one everyone wants to dance with, not me." He grinned at her. "I don't blame them either."

"You know, if you keep saying sweet stuff like that, I just might have to keep you on."

"I'm gonna hold you to that." He stepped away, pulling his shirt over his head and dumping it in the basket before searching through the wardrobe for another one. Maddi took a moment to admire his strong physique; something she could never quite get enough of. His perfectly sculpted abs mesmerised her, and no matter how often she saw them, she found herself wanting to run her fingers over the ridges.

She'd never been with another man. Ricki was her one and only, and she hoped it would always be that way. Sure, she'd dated other guys, but none that she had felt comfortable enough to share something so intimate with.

After everything that Dane had put her through, Ricki had been the perfect gentleman, never once putting pressure on her. He had waited until she was ready, and even then, he was tentative. He treated her with a gentleness she had never experienced before, making her sure that her decision had been the right one.

"Maddi?" Ricki asked, eyeing her with a cocky grin on his face. "You gonna get ready?"

"Mmhmm," she murmured under her breath, slightly embarrassed to have been caught staring. She quickly undressed, then slipped her dress on over her gentle curves. "Could you zip me up?" she asked, holding her hair in a pile on top of her head.

Ricki stepped in close, grasping the zipper in his hand and slowly pulled it up. The warmth from his fingers caused shivers to run up and down her spine.

He rested his hands on her hips and kissed the back of her neck. "You look beautiful," he whispered, his lips brushing lightly against her.

"Mmmmmm," Maddi moaned, leaning back into him.

"Oh my God, oh my God, oh my God!" Rory burst through the door, making them jump apart.

"What is it? What's happened?" Maddi asked, running to her friend.

"That was one of the judges! They loved my cake! I got in! I'm going to culinary school!" she screamed, jumping up and down. Maddi grabbed her hands and joined in.

"Oh my God! I'm so proud of you! I knew you could do it!"

"Oh-em-gee, me too!" Damon said in his best attempt at an excited teenage girl voice as he bounded into the room with them. "We should totes take a selfie to celebrate!" He pretended to flick his hair behind his shoulder and puckered his lips into something resembling 'duck face'.

Rory swatted his chest, giggling. "Geez, Damo, you're such a clown."

"That's why you love me, though, right?" He grinned at her, wiggling his eyebrows up and down suggestively.

"Yeah, yeah. I love you, ya big teddy bear." She reached up on her tippy toes to kiss him.

"I knew it!" He palmed her bottom and lifted her into his arms, wrapping her legs around his waist. "I don't know about you lot, but I'm ready to party!"

Chapter 4

Feeney's was a bar downtown, situated on one of the busiest streets. It got a lot of foot traffic, and the salsa nights were always a hit. The music was already blaring by the time they rounded the corner, and the girls couldn't help but start bopping to the beat as they walked. Now that Rory had her confirmation, she had lost her anxiety and was back to her usual bubbly self, ready to kick her heels up.

"God, I feel like it's been forever since we came out dancing!" she cried as they entered the bar. "Hurry up and change your shoes. I wanna get my dance on."

"All right, keep your shirt on," Maddi said with a grin.

"How about some drinks, ladies?" Damon asked.

"You even have to ask?" Rory raised her brow at him. "We're celebrating, remember?"

"So, two vodka and Red Bull's then?"

"You know it!" The boys made their way up to the bar to get their orders, while Rory continued to shake her body to the music. "Maaaddddiiiii, I wanna dance," she whined, tugging on her arm.

"Two secs, I've just... gotta... get this... clasp... done!" She stood up and let Rory lead her to the empty space in the centre of the room. They had the whole floor to themselves for now, and they were going to take full advantage of it.

"Let's show 'em what we got," Rory said, waving her hands at the few people still seated at their tables finishing off their meals. She broke into some sort of shimmy-type move, where she would shake her shoulders and wiggle her butt, then jump around to face another direction and repeat the process. Maddi couldn't contain her laughter as she watched her friend circle the room. She had the most intense look on her face, as if it was taking all her concentration to co-ordinate her body.

Out of the corner of her eye, she saw that the boys had put their drinks on the table and were heading out to join them. Damon immediately joined in on Rory's circular dance, mimicking her every move, but going in a counter-clockwise direction. They were the perfect match for each other—just the right amount of crazy.

"Can I have this dance?" Ricki asked, offering his hand.

"Of course." Maddi placed her hand in his and they began to sway, going through some of their favourite moves. Now that they were both teaching full time, it was nice to have these nights where they could just enjoy the music and the dance together, without it having to be about performing. This year had been rather busy preparing for the Nationals. Instead of entering as a couple though, they were focusing on their teamwork. They'd become fast friends with Nicole and Rob, the second-place winners from last year's competition, and had put together a salsa routine with them and a few other couples who'd auditioned. If they placed this year, they were planning on taking it to the World Champ's in Singapore. They had been practically living and breathing salsa for the last six months.

Of course, Maddi also had her ladies shine team to train too. They had been working on a saucy bachata number to take up to Auckland for Nationals and it was fast approaching. The Divas had been pulling some long hours, but it was all coming together nicely. In fact, they had been talking about combining the two troupes and making one big mixed team for the next year. They would just need to find a few extra men to join in to even it up.

"Don't look now, the bitch has entered the building," Rory said as she sidled up next to Maddi and nodded her head towards the door. "Looks like someone's been hitting the bottle a bit too hard." She made a drinking motion with her hand. Maddi turned to see Sacha staggering in.

"I see what you mean."

"Don't let her get to you. Just ignore her." Ricki took hold of her hand, planting a kiss on her palm.

"Sorry, she just puts me on edge."

"I know."

"The way she looks at you…"

Ricki cocked his head. "Maddi, you have nothing to worry about. She can look at me however she wants, it's not going to make me change how I feel about you." He tilted her chin up, touching his forehead to hers. "I'm not going anywhere."

Maddi sighed, letting her body relax into his. "I know. She just rubs me the wrong way. And what about Jessie? If *I* see the way she watches you, you can bet he does too."

"It's his choice to stay. He must see something in her that we don't." He shrugged. "Anyway, let's not let her ruin our night. We came here to celebrate, didn't we?" He peered down at her with a grin.

"Yes, you're right. Forget about her!" she said loudly, waving an arm in the air dismissively.

"Already forgotten." He pulled her in tight before throwing her into a series of spins around him. Their record was twelve before she began to lose balance.

"Oops," Sacha said as she stuck her foot out, making Maddi stumble. If Ricki hadn't had a hold of her still, she would've ended up in a heap on the floor. "My bad, ssooorry," she slurred.

Maddi could see Rory gearing up to cause trouble. She quickly shook her head, telling her friend not to bother with her. She then turned to Ricki and, taking his hand, she led him to another spot on the dance floor, away from Sacha's writhing body.

"We can go if you want," he said, watching her with derision in his eyes.

"No, we're not going to let her ruin our night, remember?" She reached up and pressed her lips to his. "I won't let her think she's getting to me."

"And that's why I love you."

"I love you too."

Chapter 5

Maddi scrolled through her playlist, searching for the song she wanted to use for their warm-up in class tonight. She liked to keep it interesting for her students and vary the music so they didn't get sick of hearing the same old songs. Of course, she would always have her favourites—the ones she would play every chance she got—and tonight was one of those nights. She needed to hear that familiar rhythm pumping through her veins.

The sound of cow bells filled the room as the music began to play. Without even having to think about it, Maddi began to move to the beat, her feet taking over. She and Ricki took turns running the warm-ups each week, that way they could keep it fresh and play to their strengths.

A blast of air rushed in as the door opened behind her. "Oh, sorry."

"Jessie?" Maddi pressed pause and ran over to him, throwing her arms around his neck. "How are you? Are you here for our class?"

Jessie pulled back, smiling. "Yeah, I thought I'd come and check it out, see what all the hype is about." He chuckled, looking around the room. "Where's Ricki?"

Maddi threw her arms up in the air. "I have no idea. He was meant to meet me here to go over tonight's combo." She pursed her lips, a frown creasing her forehead.

"You wanna practice with me?" he offered.

"Would you? I just need to decide what styling I'm going to add in."

"Of course. Let me get my shoes on." He sauntered over to the chairs at the edge of the studio. "It'll be nice to dance with you again, it's been a while." He looked up at her with a sadness in his eyes. Ever since he and Sacha had begun dating, it had been abundantly clear she didn't want him getting too close to Maddi.

"Yeah, it has." Maddi watched Jessie. Something wasn't quite right with him. "Are you okay?" she asked.

With a sigh, Jessie ran his hands through his hair. "That obvious, huh?" His shoulders dropped as if he was holding a huge weight on them.

Maddi walked over and sat in a vacant chair beside him. She placed her hand on his knee, peering up into his eyes. "You want to talk about it?"

He smiled at her, though it didn't quite meet his eyes. "Do I want to talk about it? Not really. Should I? Probably." He laughed nervously before meeting her gaze. "I left Sacha." He exhaled, lifting his head to stare at the ceiling.

"Aww, Jess, I'm so sorry. What happened?"

"I just couldn't be there anymore, you know? All the negativity, the cattiness." He turned to face her again. "The way she looked at other guys."

Maddi nodded her head, looking down at her lap. "Yeah, I noticed that too. I'm so sorry, Jess. I know how much she meant to you." She gave his knee a squeeze.

"Yeah, well… I can't force her to want me, so…" he trailed off, staring across the room.

"Ahem, am I interrupting something?" Ricki cleared his throat as he strolled toward them.

"Oh, hey, I didn't hear you come in. Where've you been?" Maddi asked, jumping up to greet him.

"I just had some stuff to do. Everything okay here?" He eyed Jessie warily. They'd come to an amicable friendship of sorts, though he hadn't forgotten the punch to his face a little over a year ago.

Maddi pulled him towards the front of the room. "Everything's fine. Jessie just needed a friend to talk to." She peered over her shoulder at him before whispering, "They broke up."

Ricki's eyebrow shot up. "Sacha and Jessie?" Maddi nodded. "I guess that explains her drunken state last night then."

"Mmmm, yeah I guess." She chewed the corner of her lip. "Maybe they both meant more to each other than they thought."

"Maddi," Ricki said with a warning tone. "Don't get involved. You know that Sacha will only turn it against you."

"But they're hurting," she said, looking up at him with her bright blue eyes. "And he's my friend."

Ricki let out a sigh, running his hand through his hair. "You care too much for your own good, you know that, right?" The corner of his lip curled up into a small smile.

"I know," she said, kissing his cheek. "Now, I'm going to go and have a dance with Jessie, while you get your shoes on. Class starts soon and we haven't even had a run-through." She poked a finger at his chest and attempted to give him a stern look but failed.

Ricki saluted with a grin. "Yes, ma'am."

She turned back to Jessie, who was pretending to play on his phone. "You ready for that dance?" she called, holding her hand out to him.

He looked up at her with a smile. "Just try and stop me."

Chapter 6

Rory heaved into the porcelain bowl, emptying the contents of her stomach. "I am never drinking again," she muttered, gulping in the air as she sat back against the bath, lowering her chin to her chest.

Having been so stressed out over the last few weeks while the tutors decided her fate, Rory had finally let her hair down while they were at Feeney's the night before, and she was now paying the price.

"It was those damn shots," she murmured. "Why didn't you stop me?" She squinted up at Damon who was crouching beside her.

"Baby, you only had one shot, and you were having fun, I didn't want to ruin your night for you. It was a celebration." He smiled, brushing her hair away from her face.

"Mmmm, I feel so joyous right now," she mumbled sarcastically. "Oh God…" She scrambled back to the toilet, her head hovering over the edge. "Alcohol is the devil." Her body began retching once again, ridding her stomach of whatever still remained. Damon rubbed circles on her back soothingly.

"Aaaaarrrgghhhhh," she groaned as she finally caught her breath. "Kill me, kill me now."

Damon chuckled. "I think you'll live."

She glared at him. "*You* might not."

He kissed her forehead. "Have I ever told you you're cute when you're angry?"

Rory raised an eyebrow at him, running a hand down her body in the least sexy way possible. "Are you trying to tell me you want a piece of this?"

To his credit, Damon held her gaze. "I always want you, baby." He scooped her up in his arms. "But maybe a shower wouldn't go amiss."

"Any excuse to get me naked," she said with a tired grin before running her tongue along her teeth and pulling a face. "Urgh, I need to brush my teeth too."

"Well, I didn't wanna say anything…" Damon chuckled as she slapped his chest. He set her down on the stool in the corner of the room. He opened the shower door and turned the faucet on to hot, then retrieved her toothbrush. "Here," he said, holding it out to her. "I'll go grab you a towel."

Rory slumped on the stool, slowly running the toothbrush back and forth in her mouth. She leaned her head against the wall, letting the coolness of the tiles seep through her.

"Come on, babe, let's get you into the shower," Damon said as he re-entered the room. He had a large fluffy towel and her robe draped over his arm. He set them down on the vanity, then grabbed her toothbrush from her, putting it back in the drawer. He took hold of the hem of her shirt and gently lifted it over her head, then helped her to step out of her jeans. Taking her hand, he led her to the shower and watched as she cautiously stepped under the hot stream.

"Ahhhhh," she moaned, letting the water cascade over her back as she leaned against the wall.

"You okay in there? Need any help?" Damon asked hopefully, making Rory giggle.

"You're crazy, you know that? Any other guy would be running for the hills, not rubbing my back while I blow chunks."

"Such a way with words," he said through his laughter. "Anyway, ain't no other guy gonna be watching you blow chunks but me. I'm the only one who gets that privilege."

Rory poked her head through the shower door. "Like I said—crazy." She twirled her finger by her ear and stuck her tongue out at him.

"The extremely hot kinda crazy though, right?" He put his hands on his head and began to roll his pelvis seductively at her, adding a few hip thrusts for good measure.

"Mmmhmm, definitely the hot kinda crazy," she said, her eyes dancing as she watched his little display. "Come on then." She opened the door, summoning him to join her.

"I knew you couldn't resist my charms," he said, wiggling his eyebrows at her as he tossed his clothes on the floor.

"Yeah, your 'charms'. Is that what we're calling them now?" She grinned up at him, wrapping her arms around his neck.

"You can call them whatever you want, baby." He smiled against her lips, his hands gripping onto her waist. Rory sighed, resting her head against his chest. "How you feeling now?" he asked, gently kissing the top of her head while bringing his arms around her further.

"Mmm, better, thanks."

"How much better?" he asked, going back to his hip rolling. He could feel her lips pull up into a smile.

"Trust you, Damo." She slapped his chest again.

"Hey. You can't blame a guy for trying." He ran his hands down to her bottom, palming her soft flesh and giving a squeeze. "I mean, we are naked…"

"Mmmm, yeah, we certainly are…"

"And it would be a shame to waste it…" He thrust his hips again, his length sliding across her stomach.

"Mmmm, tis true. I mean, you are getting older, and erectile dysfunction is just around the corner for you…"

"Hey!"

"Maybe you should take matters into your own hand…" She grinned up at him. "Because it ain't happening with me I'm afraid." She pressed her lips to his chest. "I would hate to blow chunks all over this here hotness." She ran her hand up and down his body.

Damon sighed. "So, I'm not getting any?"

"Not this time, buddy. Sorry," Rory said, turning around to press her body against his. "You stay in here and… ya know… do your thang." She wiggled her bottom before stepping out of the shower and grabbing her towel.

"Woman, you do not play fair sometimes," Damon complained, a groan escaping his lips as she sashayed out of the bathroom.

Chapter 7

"And five, six, seven!" Maddi called out, signalling the beginning of the move. "Basic... cross body lead, flare and booty... bring her across... switch hands as you turn..." she continued to call out instructions as they all moved to the beat. It wasn't a particularly difficult move, but putting it together with the music always proved challenging when learning a new combo.

"Break back... and comb your hands over her head..." She kept careful watch of her students, making sure that each one understood the move. She hated to move on when someone was struggling. "Good! And high five. Ladies move to the left!" They continued doing their basic step back and forth in the centre of the circle, waiting for everyone to switch partners. "From the top! And five, six, seven!"

Ricki led her through the combo, a smile on his face as he listened to her calls. His confidence had sky-rocketed after the comps the previous year, but he still wasn't as natural in front of people as Maddi was. Without her, the classes would fall apart.

One-on-one lessons with the guys was more his forte. He didn't feel so much pressure to perform in those instances and was able to relax more. In fact, he had been in discussions with a select few to form an all-male shine team. He and Rob had hit it off immediately, and between them, they had found another three guys to join them. The girls had no idea. They were planning on surprising them at the Nationals. Ricki had very nearly let the cat out of the bag on a number of occasions—keeping anything secret from Maddi was difficult, but so far, she was none the wiser.

"And high five. Ladies move to the left!" Ricki led her across so that they were facing the opposite direction. "Ladies, don't be afraid to add in your own styling. If you feel the need for a shimmy," she demonstrated against Ricki, "or a body roll, then by all means, add them in! Make it your own." She grinned, pulling herself through another cross body so she could play it up. Hoots and hollers came from around the circle as everyone cheered her on.

At first, Ricki just let her do her thing, but when he saw his chance, he broke off into his own shine steps. He may not be confident speaking to everyone, but he had the skills on the dancefloor, and he wasn't afraid to bring it. Maddi's eyes lit up as she watched him with pride.

What had begun as a demonstration had turned into a mini shine battle. "Yeow! Work it, Ricki!" one of the girls yelled out, clapping.

As the song came to an end, Ricki took charge once more and spun her over and over as he walked in a straight line through the circle, finishing by throwing her into a dip right on the final note. The class erupted into claps and cheers as they panted, smiling at each other.

Ricki pulled her back up and they took a bow. "All right let's put some music on for you guys to practice," Maddi said, walking over to where her iPod was docked. "I wanna see some originality in there, show me what you got!"

The couples all spaced out around the room, going over what they had been taught and adding in their own personal flares. Maddi and Ricki watched on from the side, checking that everyone had the move down.

"I think they've got it," he said. "Shall we?" He offered her his elbow, nodding his head to the dancefloor.

"I thought you'd never ask," she said, linking her arm through his. "Let's show 'em how it's done."

They walked out to an empty space and began to dance. "So, are you going to tell me where you keep disappearing to?" she asked, the corner of her mouth tilting up into a half-smile, as if she knew something he didn't.

"I told you, I just had some jobs to do." He avoided her eyes, knowing she would see straight through him. He wasn't sure how long he could keep lying to her.

"Oh… okay," she said, pressing her lips into a straight line. They kept dancing, but her movements became tense and mechanical. She wouldn't meet his eyes when he smiled at her.

The last thing he wanted was to upset her, but short of blowing their cover, he was out of ideas. He glanced around the room, spying Jessie sitting to one side. "Hey, why don't you go have a dance with Jessie? He looks a little lonely."

Maddi turned to see Jessie sitting on the outside, scrolling through his phone. "Okay." She dropped her arms and walked away. Something was going on with Ricki, but she couldn't figure out what. He never kept things from her.

She plonked down on the seat beside Jessie, forcing her mind to shift gears. "You know, I'm much better company than your phone," she said, draping her arms across the backs of the seats.

Chuckling, Jessie clicked his phone off and shoved it into his pocket. "Subtle, aren't you?" he said.

"Who, me?" She placed a hand to her chest, a mock look of shock on her face. "Whatever do you mean?" She held his gaze until he broke, looking away.

"I don't really wanna talk about it," he said, looking down to his feet.

"That's okay, neither do I." She winked. "I thought you might like to dance." She stood up and held her hand out to him. "Come on, you can take it out on the dancefloor."

Jessie sighed. "You never give up, do you?"

"When my friends are involved? Never." She grabbed his hand and pulled him up. "Now, let's go and help you forget about her."

Chapter 8

Rory padded down to the kitchen in the boxers and singlet she had worn to bed the night before. Her stomach was still feeling a little funny after their big night in town, and she was hoping it would settle down with a little water and some Panadol.

She was surprised to find Ricki up and dressed already. She glanced at the clock and saw that it was only 7AM. "Where are you off to this early on a Saturday morning?" she asked, stifling a yawn behind her hand.

"Just thought I'd go for a run. Couldn't sleep." He finished tying his shoes then grabbed his phone and keys off the counter. "Catch ya later," he said as he breezed past and out the door.

"Weird," she mumbled to herself as she rummaged through the drawer to find what she was looking for. Pulling an open packet out, she pressed two tablets into her palm then grabbed a glass down from the cupboard. She tipped her head back, swirling the water around her mouth as the pills slipped down her throat. She put her cup into the sink and stood, holding onto the counter with her head bowed and her eyes closed. She'd never had a hangover last so long before.

"You okay, baby?" Damon asked, coming up behind her. He placed a hand on the back of her neck and trailed it down her back.

"Yeah, I just feel a bit off still."

"You think you're coming down with something?" he asked, spinning her around to look at him. He put the back of his hand to her forehead. "You don't feel hot or anything."

"No, I'm sure I'll come right. I think I just can't handle drinking like I used to anymore. Apparently two drinks is my new limit." She attempted a weak smile.

"Maybe you should go lie down some more."

She shook her head. "No can do. My first day at *Gastronomie* is on Monday, and I need to make sure I have everything ready."

"At least let me make you some breakfast," he said. "You need a good old greasy feed of bacon and eggs. It's the perfect cure for a hangover."

"If you say so." The thought of bacon had her stomach grumbling. The eggs, not so much. "Maybe some toast too, and I have to have coffee."

"Don't you worry, I've got it covered. You go and relax." He shooed her away, busying himself with pots and pans.

Rory hovered by the counter. "I could help if you want," she offered. The kitchen was her domain usually.

"Nope, I got this. Let me look after you." He kissed the tip of her nose, then with his hands on her shoulders, he turned her towards the lounge. "Now, go and put your feet up. Read a magazine or something."

"Okay." She sighed. It wasn't easy to let go of the reigns. She liked to be the one in the kitchen feeding everyone. Let's face it, she liked being the one in *control* of the kitchen. She knew just how to make things to her liking, and she found it hard to let someone else take over. "Do you know where everything is? I don't mind helping," she tried again.

"Rory, I've lived here for almost a year. I think I know where things are by now," he said, a grin forming across his face. He knew how hard it was for her to let anyone help, but damn it, he wanted to be able to look after her too.

He had the jug boiling, the bacon in the oven and the frying pan heating by the time Maddi came out to join them.

"What's going on in here?" she asked, tying her robe around her middle.

"Damo's cooking breakfast, and he won't let me help." Rory rolled her eyes. She kept flicking through her magazine, not really paying attention to what was on the pages. Her eyes kept wandering back to the kitchen.

"Okay, I give up," Damon conceded. "Where the hell is the whisk?"

"I thought you knew where everything was?" Rory teased, her eyebrow raised.

"Third drawer down," Maddi said with a grin.

"Of course! I knew that!"

"Sure you did," Rory said.

"Quiet in the cheap seats. Breakfast will be ready soon." He brandished the whisk in the air dramatically.

"Hey, have you seen Ricki? He's not in our room," Maddi asked, joining Rory on the couch.

"Oh yeah, he was out here when I got up. Said he couldn't sleep and was going for a run?"

"Really?" Maddi screwed her nose up. "That doesn't sound like him."

"Mmm, that's what I thought too. I'm sure he'll be back soon."

Maddi leaned in closer. "Yeah. Has he seemed a little strange to you lately?" She looked at Rory, worry clouding her eyes.

"No, why? You think something's going on?"

She sat back against the couch, blowing a whoosh of air out as she did. "I don't know. He seems to be disappearing a lot. And he never tells me where he's going."

"I'm sure it's nothing. You want me to quiz Damo? Do some digging?"

"Nah, you're right. It's probably nothing." She got up from the couch, leaning on the breakfast bar. "How's breakfast coming along?"

Chapter 9

Walking along Stanmore Road to meet up with Nicole and Rob, Maddi couldn't help dragging her feet. Her thoughts kept wandering to Ricki and his behaviour of late. Disappearing at random times of the day with no explanation—this wasn't the Ricki that she knew. He loved her, of that she had no doubt, but something wasn't right. She hated to act like the jealous girlfriend who didn't trust her man, but it was getting harder and harder to ignore.

The door leading up to the studio was open when she got there. Aside from her and Lisa, Ricki was the only other one who had a key. As far as she was aware, Lisa was away for the weekend, and she couldn't think why Ricki would come down here by himself. She checked for signs of a break in, but there appeared to be none.

Cautiously, she climbed the stairs, careful not to make a sound. She peered through the window at the top of the door. Ricki was there, playing with the sound system. Maddi breathed a sigh of relief. He must've come down early to open up and crank the heaters. The studio could be freezing at this time of year.

She placed her hands on the door, about to push it open when a voice stopped her in her tracks.

"Thanks, baby," came the unmistakable drawl of Sacha.

Maddi's heart jumped into her throat as she silently watched on. Ricki turned to the right, where the bathrooms were. Sacha sauntered towards him, straightening what she was obviously trying to pass off as a skirt, but really it was more like a belt. She glanced over at the door and Maddi quickly ducked down, not wanting to be caught spying. Not when she didn't really know what she was witnessing.

Could he really be seeing Sacha behind her back? The thought made bile rush up the back of her throat. Taking a deep breath, she forced her eyes back to the window. She had to see what was going on.

Sacha was trailing a finger along the barre between her and Ricki, her ruby-red lips turned up into a sly grin. She licked her lips as she approached him, saying something that Maddi couldn't hear, no matter how much she strained her ears. She watched as Sacha ran her hand down Ricki's arm, her other hand snaking around the back of his neck, drawing him closer to her. Ricki directed his gaze to where her hand rested, but he didn't move out of her grasp. Before their lips touched, Sacha glanced back towards Maddi, winking at her. Then she smashed her lips into his, holding his face between her hands to keep him where she wanted him.

Maddi had to look away. Her throat felt constricted as she leaned her back against the wall, her head tilted back as she fought to breathe, gasping for air. When she closed her eyes, all she could see was the two of them together.

Calm down, Maddi. You've been here before. She's just trying to hurt you. He wouldn't do this.

Would he?

She didn't know what to think anymore. She needed to get out of there. She couldn't face him right now. Grabbing her bag from the floor, she quickly ran down the stairs and out into the brisk morning air. Throwing her bag over her shoulders and tucking her hands in her pockets, Maddi began to walk. She had no idea where she was going, all she knew was that she needed to get as far away from them as she could.

"Maddi?" Jessie said as he opened the door. "Is everything okay?"

"Can I come in?" she asked, her voice small and catching, as if her throat didn't want her words to escape.

"Of course." He stepped aside, ushering her into the warmth of his apartment.

"Sorry to just show up unannounced like this. I know you're still getting settled, I just didn't know where else to go." She stood awkwardly in his sparse living room.

"No, it's fine. You're always welcome here, Maddi. I'm glad you thought of me." He folded his arms across his broad chest. "I'd offer you a coffee, but I haven't bought a jug yet. It's on my list of things to do today…" A blush ran up his face, giving him a boyish look. "Here, have a seat." He rushed to pull the boxes off the couch.

"God, how rude of me. You're not even finished unpacking, and I show up crying on your doorstep," Maddi said, her face pulled into a frown.

"Seriously, Maddi, it's not a problem. You're actually doing me a favour. I was starting to go a little stir crazy. It's been so long since I've had my own place. There's so much I need to get."

"Didn't you, um, I mean, wasn't everything yours in the first place?" She couldn't bring herself to say Sacha's name. Not yet.

Jessie laughed, though the sound lacked humour. "Yeah, it was. I just didn't feel like fighting over a bunch of stuff. It was just easier to leave it there."

Maddi nodded. Sacha certainly had perfected the art of getting what she wanted.

"That's not why you're here though. Do you wanna talk about it?" he asked, repeating the same words she had said to him the night before.

"I don't know. I'm not even really sure what to say." She sighed, twisting her fingers in her lap. The sound of her phone ringing in her pocket made her jump. She pulled it out and saw Ricki's face pop up on her screen. She hit 'ignore' and shoved it back into her pocket.

"How about we start with why you're ignoring his calls, and why you came here instead of going to Rory?" He quickly added, "Not that I mind."

"I didn't want him to find me," she whispered, turning her head away as she blinked away the tears.

Jessie clenched his fists by his side. He liked Ricki, but Maddi was his friend, and he didn't like to see her hurting. He took a calming breath and crouched down in front of her.

"Maddi, what did he do?"

She sniffled. "It's like last year all over again. I saw them together."

Jessie's jaw tightened at her words. "You mean Sacha?" She simply nodded. "Where was this? What did you see, exactly?" he asked gently. He understood her anxiety all too well. It had all been a misunderstanding last time, but even knowing that, it still didn't stop it from hurting.

"Ricki was at the studio early. I was about to walk in when I heard Sacha's voice. She called him *baby*." She paused, clearing her throat. "She kissed him. And this time, it really happened. He didn't pull away."

Jessie blew out a breath. "Shit, Maddi. I don't know what to say. I mean, you know what Sacha's like. Are you sure there isn't any way you could be wrong?"

"I know what I saw, Jessie. She held his face and kissed him."

"There has to be some sort of explanation for this. I've seen the way he looks at you. There's no way he would cheat. I can see it in his eyes, he's in love with you."

"I'm not so sure anymore," she whispered. "He's been acting strange with me lately, all love and flowers one minute, and then disappearing for long periods of time without any explanation. He's hiding something from me, and I guess this is what it is."

He took hold of her hands. "I've never seen a man more in love before. Trust me, there has to be some other reason." He pulled her in for a hug. "He would never choose Sacha over you."

Chapter 10

"Sorry guys, she's not picking up. I'm not sure where she is," Ricki said, staring at his phone. He'd tried calling her three times, but each time he was sent straight to voicemail. She was avoiding him for some reason, and he wasn't sure whether to be worried or not.

"It's all right, I think we're pretty ready for Nationals anyways. We can go over our part at home, eh, Rob?" Nicole said, slinging her shoe bag over her shoulder.

"Yeah, no problem. I'm knackered after our extra rehearsal this morning anyways." Rob smiled, placing his hand on Ricki's shoulder. "She'll be right, mate. Maybe she just forgot."

Ricki nodded, though he knew she would never forget training. It meant too much to her. That, and she hated to let people down. It was one of the many things he loved about her. "Yeah, you're probably right," he said, not wanting to give them any reason to worry.

"You want a lift home?" Rob asked.

"Nah, I might just hang here for a bit, see if she shows up."

"No worries, we'll see ya Friday?"

"Yeah, of course."

"See ya then." Nicole gave him a hug and kissed his cheek. "Everything will be fine," she said quietly. "She probably just needed some time to herself. That girl does too much." She rubbed her hand up and down his arm a few times, offering a little comfort.

"Right, let's do this," Rob said, grabbing her hand and leading her out the door. "Have a good one," he called over his shoulder.

"Yeah," Ricki muttered under his breath. He checked his phone again. Still no reply to his messages. He'd give her another ten minutes and then he'd try calling again. He couldn't shake the feeling that something was wrong. It was so unlike Maddi to ignore his calls. Even more unlike her to completely disregard her friends.

"So, she hasn't been home?"

"For the last time, Ricki, no. Why would I lie?" Rory stood with her arms folded across her chest, one hip jutted out.

He looked at her incredulously. "Um, maybe because you're her best friend?" He ran his hand through his hair, grabbing the back of his neck. "Sorry, I'm just really worried about her. She's never done this before."

Rory's expression softened. "I promise you, I don't know where she is. And in all honesty, if she was trying to avoid you, she'd hardly come back home. Obviously that's the first place you're gonna look."

Ricki sighed. "Yeah, I know. I guess I just hoped I was wrong about her avoiding me."

"What'd you do anyway?" she asked.

"I have no idea. She just didn't turn up, and now her phone is switched off."

Rory pursed her lips. "Well, I know she was heading to the studio, so maybe something happened while she was on her way there?"

"Wait, so she actually said she was on her way?"

"Yeah, like two hours ago."

His mind began racing as he thought of all the possibilities. Two hours ago. Right around the time…

"Shit." He put his hands on the top of his head, his fingers threading through his hair and taking hold. "I know why she didn't show." He began to pace. "Shit!"

"Care to enlighten me?"

Dragging his hands down his face, he turned to look at her. "Sacha was there." He winced.

"Sacha? As in, bitchface, Sacha?"

He nodded his head slowly. "Yeah, her."

"Well, I mean, I know she doesn't like her, but that wouldn't stop her from training. They've faced off before." She put her hands on her hips, raising an eyebrow. "What aren't you telling me?"

"She might've kissed me."

"She what? What the hell were you thinking? Why would you let her do that?"

"I don't know! She came in saying she needed to use the bathroom, then before she left, she grabbed me and kissed me!"

"And you didn't think to push her off? Typical bloody male!" she yelled.

"She took me by surprise!"

"Oh yeah, I'm sure," she said sarcastically. "Her lips just happened to fall into yours."

"You know what she's like."

"Yeah, I do, and so do you. You never should've let her in in the first place."

"Don't you think I know that?" He paced back and forth. "What am I going to do?"

"I'll tell you what you're going to do. You're gonna go out there and look for her, and when you find her, you're going to get down on your hands and knees and beg for her forgiveness." She blocked his path, forcing him to look at her. "Don't screw this up."

"Thanks for the vote of confidence," he replied acerbically.

"I mean it. You go about this wrong, and you will lose her. You didn't see her last time. She was devastated. Now that you two are together, it is ten times worse. Be very careful what you say to her." She grabbed his arm before he could walk past. "And stop with the sneaking around. You're not doing yourself any favours."

Chapter 11

After roaming the streets for an hour, Ricki was nearly ready to give up. She obviously didn't want to be found. He'd tried calling the girls from her dance troupe, but no one had seen her. He stopped on the corner, leaning up against a lamp post while he scrolled through his phone again, hoping for a name to jump out at him.

"Jessie, of course," he mumbled to himself as he put the phone to his ear.

"Ricki," came Jessie's abrupt voice.

"Jessie, hi," Ricki began, suddenly nervous. "I… ah… don't suppose you've seen Maddi? She didn't show up for practice today, and she won't answer my calls." He hung his head, hating to have to admit that to him.

"Yeah, I've seen her."

"Oh, thank God! Is she okay? Can I talk to her?"

"She's not here. She left about fifteen minutes ago."

"Oh, okay. Umm…"

"Why'd you do it, man?"

Unsure what she had told him, he answered, "Do what?"

"You know what I'm talking about. Why'd you kiss Sacha?"

Ricki sighed, running his hand through his hair. "I didn't mean for it to happen. She caught me by surprise."

"Well, Maddi thinks you're cheating on her. She saw you kiss, and she didn't see you pull away. She said you've been sneaking around too. What's that about?" Jessie demanded.

"I haven't been sneaking…"

"Look, if you're not going to be honest with her, then just end it," he interrupted. "Take it from me, Sacha only looks out for number one. She doesn't care about anyone else. Maddi is one of the sweetest girls I've ever met. Don't string her along. She deserves better than that."

"She deserves the world! I swear to you, Jessie, I am not cheating on her. I would never do that to her. I love her."

"I want to believe you, man. I do. But it's not looking good."

"I was going to propose!" Ricki blurted out.

"Wait, what?"

"The sneaking about? I've been planning to propose when we go up to Auckland for the Nationals. I've got this whole routine planned out around it. I thought it would be romantic. I never meant for any of this to happen. Please, Jessie, you've gotta help me. I can't lose her," Ricki pleaded.

"Shit," Jessie huffed down the phone. "Well, at least *that* I can believe." He paused, thinking. "Does it have to be done in Auckland?"

"No, I guess not."

"Okay, it's Saturday night, there will be dancing somewhere. Let me check around and I'll get back to you. Be ready to propose tonight."

"She won't even talk to me, Jessie. How is this going to work?"

"I'll make sure she's there, you just worry about this routine you've got planned. Please tell me Sacha isn't involved in it?"

"Of course not!"

"I just had to check. I may be able to get her to hear you out, but I'm no miracle worker," he joked.

Ricki couldn't believe what Jessie was doing for him. They'd had their moments, but when it came down to it, Jessie really was a good guy. It was no wonder Maddi thought so highly of him.

"Hey, Jessie?"

"Yeah?"

"Thanks. I know we never really got off on the right foot… I just really appreciate your help."

"Hey, it's like I said, Maddi is the sweetest girl I've ever met, and she deserves to be happy. If I can be a part of that, then I'm happy to help. Now, I'm going to head out. I'll text you with the venue."

Disconnecting the call, Ricki shoved his phone back in his pocket, a nervous thrill running through his body. He was going to propose tonight.

He was going to propose *tonight*. Holy shit.

Drumming his fingers on the table while his knee bobbed up and down nervously, Ricki sat watching the door, waiting for Jessie to show up. He had text him the venue and had even spoken to the manager to arrange their little presentation.

Ricki had spent the afternoon with Rob and the guys, rearranging their routine to fit with the smaller space. He had pulled the little square box out of his pocket so many times, just to check that it was still there. He wanted everything to be perfect.

"You look like you could use one of these," Rob said, placing a bourbon in front of him.

"Thanks," Ricki said, wrapping his hand around the glass. "I've never been more nervous in my life."

"You two are crazy about each other. What are you so worried about?" he asked.

"That she doesn't show up, that she says no, that I forget the ring…" He palmed his pocket once more just to be sure.

"You've got the ring, I've seen you staring at it all day, and she's going to say yes, so don't worry, man. Have a drink, it'll calm your nerves."

Nodding, Ricki lifted the glass to his lips, taking a large gulp.

"Better?"

"Mmhmm," he murmured, turning his attention back to the door. He had given in and told Rory what was going on so that she and Damon would convince Maddi to come out tonight. *God, what if she's so mad at me that she doesn't show?*

He checked his watch; half an hour until they were on. Where were they? He could feel the sweat beginning to form on his brow as he considered the thought that she might not come.

He grabbed his drink and finished it in one mouthful. Standing, he muttered to Rob that he was going to the bathroom before staggering across the room. He pushed through the door and was relieved to see that he was alone. He went to the sink and turned the tap, cupping his hands underneath. Splashing the cool water on his face, he lifted his head to stare at his reflection in the mirror. "Get a hold of yourself. She'll be here." After a beat, he pulled a paper towel from the holder and held it to his face, soaking up the moisture. With one last look in the mirror, he crumpled the paper into a ball and threw it in the bin.

Stepping out of the bathroom and back into the bar, he couldn't stop his eyes from travelling to the door once more. His breath caught in his throat when he was met with the icy-blue gaze of Maddi. She was finally here.

Chapter 12

"It wasn't easy, but I convinced her to come. Don't worry, I haven't let the cat out of the bag. She thinks we're here to see Nicole perform her solo," Rory said as she sidled up to Ricki's side.

"Thanks, Rory. It means a lot." He smiled nervously at her. "You want a drink?"

Screwing her face up, Rory quickly shook her head. "Not for me thanks. I'm still recovering from the other night." She rubbed her stomach as if the thought alone made her queasy. "Can't be showing up to class all hungover anyways."

"Yeah, probably not the best look on your first day." Ricki blew out a breath, wiping his hand across his brow before patting his pocket once again. "God, I'm so nervous."

Rory slapped her hand on his shoulder. "I know she's pissed at you right now, but she'll get over it. She loves you, man."

"I hope so. I don't want to lose her."

"Just work your magic. I know she can't resist your bangin' moves on the dancefloor." She turned her body, leaning her back against the bar. "I'd better get back to her. Can't have her getting all suspicious now, can we?"

Ricki nodded his head, bringing his drink to his lips for a bit of Dutch courage. It was almost time.

"Bitch alert," Damon said as he came up to the bar.

"You've got to be kidding me."

"Nope, sorry. She looks wasted again, too."

"Son of a bitch. Just what I need right now," Ricki huffed. "Has Maddi seen her?"

"Not yet, but it's only a matter of time."

Plastering what he hoped was a charming smile on his face, Ricki stepped away from the bar.

"Where are you going?"

"Damage control." He stalked over to the table where Maddi and Rory were sitting, watching the dancers on the floor. "Ahem, Maddi?" he started. "Would you like to dance?" He held his hand out to her, silently praying that she would accept.

"Ricki…"

"Please? Just one dance? You don't even have to talk to me if you don't want to." He wasn't above begging if it meant she would be in his arms again. "It's our song," he said softly. She sighed, gingerly placing her hand in his.

"One dance," she said, avoiding his eyes.

He led her to the dancefloor and pulled her into a closed position, careful to leave a little space between them. Just the fact that she was allowing him this dance made him feel more at ease. Maybe, just maybe, she would forgive him. But would she say yes? Part of him felt like it was silly to ask her now, while she wasn't talking to him. The rest of him wanted to do anything to have her back in his arms for good.

As the song went on, Maddi slowly relaxed into him as she pressed her cheek to his chest. A contented sigh left her lips, and he took that as a sign that things would be okay. He pressed his arm into her back, pulling her against him. She didn't resist.

One song led into another, and Maddi made no move to leave. She even managed a smile as she broke into a shine.

"Woooh! My turn," Sacha slurred as she twirled through the dancefloor, colliding with Maddi and sending her crashing to the floor. Before Ricki could help her up, Sacha had latched onto his arm for balance.

"What the fuck are you doing, Sacha?" he cried incredulously.

"Taking what's mine," she snarled, slamming her lips into his. Ricki gripped her shoulders and pushed her off him.

"Jesus, stop!"

"What? You don't wanna piece of this?" She ran her hands up and down her body, pursing her lips seductively.

"No, Sacha, I don't want any piece of you! I want Maddi!" He spun around to grab her from the floor, but she was gone. "Fuck!"

"Whassa matter, big boy? Your girl can't handle a bitta competition?" Sacha sneered.

"What the hell is wrong with you? There *is* no competition! Even if there was, Maddi would win hands down every time! She's the one for me. Get it through your head!" He turned on his heels and marched off the dancefloor, his eyes scanning the crowd for Maddi.

"She's gone, mate," Damon said from behind. "Come on, I'll help you look for her."

"Don't you ever get tired of messing with people?" Jessie said as he came up beside Sacha.

"What? I'm juss havin' some fun. 'snot my problem if they can't handle the jandal." She erupted into a fit of giggles. "Handle the jandal," she repeated with a snort.

"You're drunk," he stated with a sigh.

"So? What's your point? Why d'you even care?" she slurred, stumbling into him. She relaxed into his chest for a few seconds before pushing away. She turned her eyes brimmed with tears to his. "We're not together anymore, remember?"

"I still care about you, Sacha. You know that. But what you just did? That was beyond cruel. You're toying with their relationship."

She waved a dismissive hand. "Pfft, whatever. She'll get over it."

"I don't know if she will. After that stunt you pulled this morning, and now this little display, you can't blame her for being upset."

"An' this is my problem because…" She folded her arms across her chest defiantly.

"You made it your problem when you decided to play your games. She thought he was cheating on her, but he was going to propose tonight," he said softly. "You can't keep doing this to people."

"Wait… He… He was going to propose?" she whispered, her hand flying to her mouth as she blinked away the tears that sprang to her eyes. No one had ever wanted her enough to propose before, except maybe Jessie, and she'd pushed him away. Her stupid antics to make him jealous had backfired, and short of throwing herself at him, she didn't know what else to do. "I didn't know…"

"I know you didn't. But this is why you can't go around messing with people's heads."

"I can fix it…" She scanned the room, hoping to find Maddi so she could explain. "Lemme fix it."

"You need to leave them alone. Give them their space." He paused, his earlier anger now replaced with pity. "I know you, Sacha. Even though you tried to hide it, when we were together, I saw glimpses of the real you, the vulnerable you." He cupped his finger and thumb under her chin, tilting her head up to look at him again. "Find what makes you happy. Maybe then you'll stop hurting others." He brushed his lips across her forehead before walking away.

No longer able to conceal her tears, they slowly slid down her cheeks as she watched him leave, her fingers held to her lips. "You made me happy," she whispered.

Chapter 13

"Same 'gain," she said, slamming a twenty down on the bar. Her sorrows were slowly dimming as the alcohol took over her system, numbing the pain.

"I think you've had enough, Miss," the bartender replied, pushing her money back.

"Nope, I don' thinkso." Sacha pursed her lips in an attempt to be sexy. "Jus' one more." She held her finger in the air.

"Sorry, I can't serve you any more alcohol tonight."

"Fine. I'll fin' someone who will." She stumbled away from the bar, falling into a group of guys. She giggled, grabbing a muscled bicep to hold herself up. "Sorry." She giggled again. Her mother's words from long ago, rang in her ears, *"You, my girl, have been blessed with boobs and a booty that men will find irresistible. Show 'em a bit of skin, a good time in the bedroom, and you'll want for nothing..."* Puffing her chest out, she leaned into her muscular friend and gave him a wink. "Buy me a drink?" she purred, licking her lips.

"Sure thing, baby. What are ya drinking?"

"Whateveryou're buyin'."

"That's my kinda girl." He palmed her arse, giving a squeeze on his way past. "Don't you go anywhere."

Sacha stood there, swaying out of time to the music. Her vision was starting to blur, and she was finding it harder to stand up straight. Staggering backwards, she caught hold of a chair to steady herself while she waited for her new friend.

"Here ya go, sexy," he said, holding a tall glass out to her.

Sacha took hold of the drink, her tongue darting out to find the straw. She drew in a few quick mouthfuls.

"Mmmm, delishishis…delishish…delicious," she slurred, again breaking into giggles. "Oops!" She fell against the chair that had been holding her up, tipping it into the table and in turn, spilling several drinks.

"Here ya go." One muscular arm wrapped around her waist, helping her to stand, while the other retrieved the teetering chair before it clattered to the floor. "Maybe we should sit down." He swung the chair away from the table and sat, bringing her onto his lap. "That's better."

"Mmmmm, much." Sacha leaned into his hard chest, nuzzling her head into the crook of his neck, pretending it was Jessie. She brought her glass up, this time deciding to do without the straw, and took a big gulp.

"You like that?"

"Mmmhmm," she murmured, her lips still wrapped around her glass.

"Plenty more where that came from." He ran his hand down from her waist to her thigh, resting it there.

"'Sat right?" she asked, tipping her head back to finish it off. She held the glass up in front of her, wiggling it side to side. "Finnnnisssshhhhed," she sang.

"Hey, Mike! Grab us another drink, would ya?" He handed his friend some money. "Make hers a double." He winked, edging his hand further around her thigh, his fingertips trailing back and forth.

"'snuffa that," she muttered, picking his hand up and moving it back to her waist. "Don' wanna giveyer frien's a show," she garbled, waving her hand about in front of her. "'saint no peep show." Her hand dropped down onto her lap as she fell back against him, her eyes struggling to focus. "I don' feelsogood."

"You'll be right. You just need something to drink, that's all." Mike had returned with their drinks, and he promptly thrust one in her face. "Drink up, love."

"Jus' a lil bit." She tried to reach for the glass, but the room was beginning to spin and she couldn't see straight. Her hand just flailed about in front of her.

"Here." He put the straw into her mouth. "Suck."

"Mmmhmm." She did as she was told, though it wasn't making her feel any better. What she really wanted to do was go home to bed. Pushing the glass away, she attempted to push up off his lap.

"Woah there. Steady on, let me help you."

"Immmmmokay, I candoit," she said, but his grip around her waist tightened.

"I said, let me help you." He quickly stood up, still holding her against his side. "Sure you don't want more of that drink?" he asked.

She wrinkled her nose. "Nope," she popped the P, letting her eyes close and her head lean into him. "I jus' needta…" She fluttered her eyes open again, trying to stay focused. "I… think…I needagohome… ta'bed."

"Sure thing, sweet cheeks. Lead the way."

She let him hold her up, taking the majority of her weight as she stumbled through the crowd. When they burst through the doors and she was hit with the cool night air, she started to feel a little better. She looked up at the hulking guy beside her. He seemed nice enough, but did she really want to be going home with him? She'd been with Jessie so long, it seemed strange to be in this situation again.

Jessie.

She turned her head, searching for his face amongst the throngs of people, unsure if she wanted to find him or not. The thought of him seeing her in this state didn't sit well with her. Despite what he thought, she really did love him. *God, please don't let him have seen me like this.*

Her mind made up, she placed her hand on his chest to stop him. "I'm jus' gonna calla taxi," she said, pushing away from him.

"No need, babe. I can drive us back to mine." He pulled a set of keys out of his pocket and jingled them in front of her.

Frowning, Sacha poked her finger at him. "You can't drive."

"Sure I can." He grinned at her, his arm snaking around her waist and drawing her back into his side. "Trust me." He kissed the top of her head, giving her middle a squeeze, his thumb brushing back and forth against the underside of her breast.

Sacha waited for the feeling of self-worth to fall over her as it so often had in the past when she had the attention of a man, but it didn't come. Instead she was left feeling disgusted. A chill ran down her spine as she realised what a mistake she was making.

"I don'wanna…" she said, prying his fingers away from her.

"Come on now. I'm just having some fun," he taunted, placing his hand further up so he was now cupping her.

Panic began setting in, sobering her somewhat. "I said don't," she managed, as she tried to wrench his hand off her, but he only held on tighter, hurting her. She looked around for someone who could help her.

"We're all alone here, sweet cheeks. Come on, let's have some fun." He smirked as he dragged her around the corner into darkness.

"Sorry, mate. That was Rory. Maddi's going home and… she doesn't want to see you."

"Of course she doesn't. I've really fucked things up this time, Damo. I don't know why I tried to do something so over the top. It's not who I am." Ricki ran his hand through his hair in frustration. "I should've just proposed when I had the chance, without all the theatrics."

"You'll get through this. Maddi's a reasonable girl, and she loves you. She'll hear you out once she's calmed down."

"I hope you're right." Shoving his hands in his pockets, Ricki stopped to suss out their whereabouts. "May as well head back. Do you think it'd be okay if I sleep on the couch?"

"It's your place too," Damon said, shrugging. "And mine. I'm sure she'll be over it by the morning."

As they rounded the corner to take them back to Feeney's, a movement in the shadows caught his eye. Nudging Ricki, he nodded toward the darkness. "Is it just me, or does that look like a couple making out?"

Ricki followed his gaze, squinting his eyes to focus. "Is that… Sacha?"

"You know, I think you may be right."

A crease formed on his brow as he continued to watch. "I don't feel good about this. She's not moving, I don't think she's conscious. And who is that guy she's with?"

"Certainly not anyone we know." Damon flexed his hands into fists.

Ricki turned to Damon with a look of concern. "I'm probably going to regret this, but we should do something."

"You don't have to ask me twice." He tilted his head side-to-side, cracking his neck. "For the record, this is why Maddi will come back to you. Even after all the shit Sacha has caused you, you're still willing to help her when she's in need. You're a better man than most." He squared his shoulders, pushing his shirt sleeves up. "Now, let's go sort this shithead out."

Chapter 14

"He was going to propose?" Maddi stopped walking, turning to face her friend. "Seriously?"

Rory nodded her head. "Yup. That's what all the sneaking around was about. He had this big elaborate thing planned for in Auckland, but you know, shit happened today, so he brought it forward. Jessie helped him organise it."

"I had no idea," she said softly.

"You and me both. The only reason he told me was so that I would make sure you came tonight." She reached out, grasping Maddi's hands. "What you saw in there? That was just Sacha being Sacha. Ricki is head over heels in love with you, girl. Always has been."

Maddi searched Rory's eyes, knowing she would never lie to her. Letting out a sigh, she brought her hands to her face, then slowly peeled her fingers open to peer through.

"Okay, maybe you're right. We need to go back and find him."

Rory beamed. "That's my girl!" She let out an excited squeal. "I'm gonna be a bridesmaid!" She latched onto Maddi's elbow, practically dragging her down the road and back into town.

"Hey!" Damon roared as they approached the couple in the shadows.

"Sacha?" Ricki called out. "You okay?"

"She's fine, mate. We're just leaving."

"Sacha?" Ricki tried again.

"Back off and get your own date," the guy growled.

"We're not letting you take her anywhere," Damon spat. "What's the matter, *mate*? Can't get a sober girl to go home with you, so you have to resort to dragging a comatose one down a dark alley?" He puffed his chest out as he stepped in front of the guy.

"Who the fuck do you think you are, tough guy?" the guy snarled, letting go of Sacha and moving to within an inch of Damon's face. They both stood there glaring at each other, daring the other to make the first move.

"Sacha? Can you hear me?" Ricki asked, cradling her head against his chest. "Sacha? Come on, I need you to wake up now."

"Mmmmmhmmmpffff," she mumbled.

"That's a girl, open your eyes for me," Ricki said, gently rocking her in his arms. Looking over at Damon and the guy's stare off, he cleared his throat, directing his next words their way. "What did you give her?"

"I didn't give her anything."

Damon narrowed his eyes. "Try again, mate. What did you give her?" He spoke slowly, articulating each word.

"I told you, I didn't give her anything. I just bought her a couple drinks. It's not my fault if she can't handle her alcohol," he sneered, shoving Damon, whose large frame barely even moved.

"Tut tut," Damon said, shaking his head with a glint in his eye. "Everyone knows you don't make the first move." Flattening his hands against the guy's chest, he pushed, sending him backwards. "Now you're fair game. Self-defence and all that." He stalked towards him, fists clenched at his sides.

Meanwhile, Ricki had one arm wrapped securely around Sacha's back, holding her up while he cupped her face in his other hand. "Come on, Sacha. Talk to me. What did he do to you?"

Her brow furrowed and she whimpered, bringing her arms up between them as if to push him away.

"Shhh, Sacha, it's me. It's Ricki." He began to stroke her face, trying to calm her. "I'm not going to hurt you."

"Ricki?" she mumbled, her eyes fluttering as she tried to open them. "I'm so sssorry," she slurred before passing out. Ricki scanned the area for a place to sit her down. Spotting an empty doorway down the road, he quickly walked her over, leaving Damon to sort out the douchebag.

"Here we go, let's take a seat." He eased their bodies down to the step, cushioning her body against his, her head resting on his shoulder. He wrapped an arm around her, pulling her shaking body in close to keep her warm. With the light from the lamp post beside them, he took a moment to scan over her, searching for any signs of harm. Her dress was torn but still intact, and her hair had matted in a sticky mess to one side. As gently as he could, he brushed her hair aside to find a large gash just above her ear. "Shit." A shudder ran through him at the thought of what might've happened. "Sacha, I need you to wake up for me," he said again, rubbing his hand up and down her arm. "Come on, open your eyes."

A scuffle to the side caught his attention as Damon hauled the guy over, his hands twisted behind his back. His eye was swelling shut, and a trickle of blood ran down from the corner of his mouth. "You got your phone on you? We should call the cops and report this guy," he said, barely even out of breath.

"Yeah, hang on, it's in my pocket." Ricki shifted his weight, Sacha's head lolling forwards. "Shit," he cussed under his breath, trying to hold her up and reach for his phone at the same time.

"Ricki?" Maddi's small voice came from across the road.

"Maddi?" he called out.

"What's going on?" she asked as she made her way over to them, eyeing up the battered man in Damon's arms. "What did you do?" It was then that she saw Sacha practically in Ricki's lap. Her eyes went wide as they darted between the three of them. "What happened? Is she okay?"

"Is that Sacha?" Rory asked, squatting down beside Ricki to get a better look. "She doesn't look too good."

"No, she's not. We need to call an ambulance and the cops, do either of you have a phone on you?" Ricki's voice sounded calmer than he felt.

"On it," Rory said, snatching her phone out of her purse. "What am I telling them?"

"We caught this guy dragging her off down that alley over there," he nodded down the street a bit. "She wasn't moving, and I think maybe he drugged her. I can't get her to wake up."

Maddi clasped her hands to her mouth, shaking her head side-to-side as tears came to her eyes. Her breath came out in pants as she stumbled backwards.

Ricki knew how hard this must be for her to see after what Dane had put her through the year before. "Maddi, it's okay. She's going to be okay. He didn't have a chance to… ya know… He didn't… We got to her in time." He held her gaze, willing her to stay with him and not regress back to the shell of a woman she had been for a time after her attack.

Sacha's body began to twitch in his arms, causing him to look away. Her jaw clenched tight as her eyelids fluttered open, her eyes rolling backwards. A thin trail of spittle ran down her chin as her body started convulsing fiercely.

"Shit! She's having a seizure!" Ricki yelled, struggling to keep her from falling to the concrete. "Maddi, I need your help!" When she didn't move, he shouted again, "Maddi! Help me!"

As if a switch had been turned on, she blinked once, then ran to his side, cradling Sacha's head in her arms as they lay her jerking body across both of their laps.

"Ambulance is on the way!" Rory called, settling herself on the step below them to help. "Don't hold her too tight. I read somewhere that you're not meant to try and stop them, or they can hurt themselves." Placing a hand on both their knees, Rory formed a barrier so that Sacha couldn't fall from her perch, and they could loosen their hold. Within minutes, the seizure had subsided. "We need to get her onto her side and check her airway. I think she's better off lying on the concrete."

Between the three of them, they eased her down to the ground and into the recovery position while they waited for the ambulance to arrive. Damon continued to hold her attacker, twisting his hands just that little bit further up behind his back, making him cry out in pain.

"What's that? Am I hurting you?" Damon said, dragging him closer to Sacha. He grabbed him by the hair and forced him to look at her. "See what you did?" he demanded. "She's half your size, you worthless piece of shit. Did that stop you?"

"I'm sorry," he stuttered, wincing as his arms were bent even more.

"Damon," Ricki cautioned, nodding towards the girls who were trying to make Sacha comfortable by rolling a jacket up and sliding it under her head. The distant sound of sirens let them know that help was finally on the way, so Rory got to her feet and jogged out to the corner to wave them down.

"You're going to be okay, Sacha," Maddi crooned softly while stroking her hair. "You're going to be okay."

Chapter 15

"Where is she?" Jessie ran up to the reception desk. "Sacha Barrett, she was brought in here, I need to see her."

"Jessie," Maddi called, beckoning him over to the waiting room. She stood, her arms held out in front of her, offering comfort. Without hesitation, Jessie threw himself into her arms, grasping onto her as if his life depended on it. She just held him, slowly running her hand up and down his back soothingly. Little by little, he felt the tension begin to wane. Pulling back, he looked into her eyes, searching for some kind of solace.

"What happened? Is she... is she okay?" he whispered.

"Come and sit down," Maddi urged, taking hold of his hand and leading him to one of the seats away from prying eyes. "They haven't really told us much, I guess because we're not family. All we know is that she has been rushed into surgery. She had bleeding on the brain, and they needed to do something to relieve the pressure."

The colour drained from his face as he stared at her in disbelief. "This can't be happening," he murmured, swiping his hand across his eyes. "I was talking to her not long ago, she was fine. A little drunk, but fine. How did this happen?" he asked.

Ricki cleared his throat. "We found her," he motioned to Damon, who was sitting to his left, his arms wrapped around Rory. "This guy had been feeding her drinks, maybe something else too, we're not sure. He was trying to drag her down an alley when we saw them. She was out to it." He paused, not wanting to overwhelm him any more than needed. "She had a cut above her ear," he pointed to his own head, "probably from trying to get away. At least that's what the cops thought."

Jessie hunched over, his elbows planted on his knees and his face in his hands. "I shouldn't have left her," he muttered. "She was upset and drunk, and I left her to fend for herself."

"This isn't your fault, Jessie." Maddi knelt in front of him, making him look at her. "No one could have known. The main thing is that they got to her before he had a chance to take it any further."

His head snapped up. "So, she wasn't…"

Maddi shook her head. "No. It didn't get that far."

Turning his tear-filled eyes to Ricki, he nodded his head. "Thank you," he managed. "Both of you. I don't know what I would've done…"

"Shhh, don't do that to yourself," Maddi soothed. "She's safe now. That's all that matters."

"If it makes you feel any better, I got a couple of punches in before the cops arrived," Damon said, a smirk on his face as he recalled the satisfying crunch of the guy's nose.

Jessie scoffed, his lips pulling up in the faintest of smiles. "Thanks, that actually does make me feel a little better."

"He's lucky I can control my temper. It wasn't easy though."

"You're a stronger man than I. I would've ripped his fucking head off," Jessie spat the last part out, his jaw locked in a grimace.

"Believe me, if I didn't have this one to go home to," he pulled Rory in close, "I probably would have." He kissed the top of her head. "I just didn't fancy being locked up while he got off scott free."

"He won't, will he?" Rory questioned. "Get off scott free I mean." She peered up at Damon, a shudder running down her spine. "Just the thought of him out on the streets gives me the heebie jeebies."

Maddi, who had gone back to her seat, was staring at her hands in her lap.

"You okay?" Ricki asked softly, placing his hand on top of hers.

"Mmhmm." She nodded, but he could see the tears slowly trickling down her cheeks. Bringing his hand up to cup her face, he gently brushed them away with his thumb.

"You're thinking about Dane, aren't you?" he said knowingly.

A small sigh escaped her lips as she glanced up at him. "I know it's wrong, we're meant to be here for Sacha…" she trailed off, looking back down at their hands entwined.

"It's okay to feel this way, Maddi. What you went through was traumatic, and there are definite similarities here. It's no wonder it's brought those memories back to the forefront."

Nodding her head, she said, "I guess." Frowning, she added, "I was so scared. For a minute there, I thought you and her were… and then when I realised… I just kept having flashes of his face above me."

"Come here," he said, pulling her onto his lap. "It's okay. You know I will never let him get close to you again, right?"

"I know," she whispered.

"And, for the record, you're the only girl I want in my arms." He tilted her chin up, pressing his forehead against hers. "It's always been you." Those words alone were enough to open the floodgates. Unable to hold back any longer, she buried her face into the crook of his neck, sobbing while he cradled her against him.

An hour later, a short, balding man garbed in blue scrubs came barrelling through the doors and into the waiting room. "Mrs Barrett?" he asked.

Jessie jumped up. "I haven't been able to get hold of her."

"And you are?"

"Jessie, sir." He held his hand out. "I'm her… she was my… we're best friends," he said, stumbling through his words.

Ricki strode over to join them. "You're the doctor who worked on her?" he asked.

"Yes, I am. Is anyone here related to Miss Barrett?"

Jessie shook his head. "No, we're not. She hasn't seen her father since she was a baby, and her mother, well, let's just say they're not really on speaking terms," he explained. He motioned to the group around him as he said, "We're really all she has."

Nodding, the doctor said, "Well, it's not normally how we like to do things around here, but I can see how much she must mean to you all, and I'd rather she had some support while she recovers." He paused, looking each of them in the eye before continuing. "The bleed was more severe than we first thought and the amount of alcohol in her system hasn't helped. Her brain has been through a considerable amount of trauma this evening, so we've had to put her into an induced coma. She's being taken through to recovery as we speak."

"Can we see her?" Jessie asked, folding his arms across his broad chest.

"Not just yet. I'll have a nurse let you know when she's been moved into a room. I'd prefer that you limit it to one person at a time to start with. She's going to be under for at least 24 hours, maybe longer."

"But she'll be okay though?" Jessie asked.

"It's really up to her now, son. We've done all that we can for her for now." He clapped a hand on his shoulder. "She's a fighter, and she's got some great support with you here. Just try to stay positive. Talk to her, let her know you're all here for her."

"Yes, sir," Jessie said, nodding his head. "Thank you, for everything."

"No need to thank me. I'm just doing my job."

"Even so, I'm glad you're here to do it." Jessie shook his hand again. "I couldn't bear to lose her."

The doctor gave a sympathetic look. "She's still got a long road to go. Hang in there."

Chapter 16

"Why don't you guys go home and get some rest?" Jessie suggested as Rory curled up in a ball on the couch, her head tucked into her chin. "The doctor said she'll be under for a while, no point in all of us losing sleep."

"Nah, we're good," Rory said with a yawn.

"Look at you, you can barely keep your eyes open." Turning to Damon, he said, "Just take her home, honestly, I'm fine to stay here with Sacha."

"You sure?"

"Absolutely. You guys have already done so much for her. I can't thank you enough for what you did tonight." He shook his head in disbelief. "I still can't believe this has happened. It's like some sort of nightmare, you know? You hear of these stories, but you never expect it to happen to someone you're close to."

Ricki and Maddi exchanged a look. She knew he wanted to say something, but now wasn't the time. She gave a small shake of her head, letting him know how she felt. She saw his shoulders lift and fall as he suppressed a sigh.

When Dane had forced himself on her last year, she hadn't wanted anyone to know. Other than Ricki, Damon and Rory, who had come to her rescue, no one else had been told. Word had spread through the dance community of Dane's arrest, but the details had been vague. Of course, there had been whispers, but Ricki had been quick to shut them down, knowing how Maddi wanted to keep it quiet.

He couldn't understand it really. When he'd walked in and seen her pinned to the bed with a vacant look in her eyes, he'd very nearly lost it. As far as he was concerned, Dane deserved to be dragged through the wringer. He felt that the dance community needed to know what kind of person he was. Maddi, on the other hand, just wanted to forget it had happened in the first place. She couldn't bear the thought of people pitying her or feeling as though they needed to tip-toe around her.

Directly after the attack, she had hidden herself away, only feeling comfortable around the three of them. It hadn't been until the night of the comps when she had finally stepped out of her comfort zone and gone out. It had taken some convincing, but once she was immersed into the dance world once more, it was as if a weight had been lifted from her shoulders. She had blossomed, becoming an even stronger dancer and mentor for others. What she'd been through, he wouldn't wish on anyone, but he had to admit, it had made her a stronger person. The change had been subtle, and only those close to her had really noticed it.

Maddi had this light inside her that shone brighter than anything he'd ever seen before. People were drawn to her. Not only was she mesmerizing to watch, she was also humble, and that made people want to be around her. It was inevitable that they would begin teaching their own classes alongside Lisa.

Watching her now, he knew she was hurting from the reminder, but he could still see that light behind her eyes. He would do anything to keep that light shining bright, and if it meant he had to keep it in and not divulge her secret to Jessie, then so be it.

Turning his attention back to Jessie, he acknowledged what he'd said. "Yeah, it was pretty scary to see." Shoving his hands in his pockets, he caught Maddi's eye, trying to convey his understanding to her. "I'm just glad we could help. She's going to need a lot of support to get through this."

Rubbing the back of his neck, Jessie glanced up from the floor, an odd expression on his face. "Look, I know you guys haven't always seen eye to eye," he raised his hand to stop them from saying anything before he continued, "and I know that it's her doing. I just… what you're doing, by being here? It really means a lot. It's no excuse, but she hasn't had an easy life. I know she puts on this tough front, but her folks aren't really around, and as you know, she's not the best at making friends or letting people in." He toed the ground, taking a deep breath. "I know you don't have to be here…"

Maddi put her hand on his arm. "It's okay, Jessie. We want to be here. For both of you."

His shoulders sagged with her words. "You have no idea how much that means to me."

"It's what friends do." She smiled. "And even though you both won't admit it, I know you love each other." She looked over at Ricki with a grin. "It's kinda something we know a bit about."

Reaching out to take her hand, Ricki added, "You know she's right; she always is."

"I think maybe, when you go in to see her, you should tell her how you feel. I mean, it's the perfect time, don't you think?"

"At least she can't run away," Damon added as he scooped Rory into his arms.

"Damo! That's not what I meant," Maddi scolded.

"It can't hurt though, right?" Ricki said with a tip of his head. "Don't they say that you can still hear everything going on around you while you're in a coma? Might give her some incentive to wake up."

"Exactly," Maddi said, nodding.

"Or…"

"Damo!" both Maddi and Ricki said.

"Okay, okay! Just trying to lighten the mood." He walked towards the door. "I'm going to head home and get this one into bed." He waggled his eyebrows suggestively.

"Go!" Maddi giggled, pointing out the door.

"Fine, I'm going." He looked at Ricki, holding his hand up and wiggling his thumb around as if typing. "Let me know if you need anything."

"Will do."

As soon as he'd passed through the door, a nurse poked her head into the room. "Sacha has been moved into her own room now if you would like to sit with her for a little while."

Jessie practically ran to the door. "Yes please, I'd like to see her."

Smiling warmly, the nurse stepped aside, allowing him to join her. "Okay, follow me."

Chapter 17

Standing at the edge of the room, Jessie watched Sacha's chest slowly rise and fall. He had never seen her look more vulnerable than at this moment. Along one arm, a handprint was visible in shades of blue and purple. The stark white bandage adorning her head stood in sharp contrast to her jet-black hair, making her seem almost angelic.

Struggling to hold back tears, Jessie cautiously stepped into the room, edging closer to the bed. His hand hovered above hers tentatively, scared he might hurt her.

"You can touch her," the nurse said from the doorway. "You won't break her, I promise. It might even help her to feel you with her."

Jessie nodded appreciatively. Turning back to Sacha, he eased her hand into his, giving a gentle squeeze to let her know he was there.

"Hey, beautiful," he whispered. "I'm so sorry I wasn't there for you." He sat down, burying his face in her sheets and pressing kisses to the back of her hand. "I'd do anything to take it back. I never should have left you." His resolve shattered and he was no longer able to hold back the tears. A sob escaped as he raised a hand to stroke her face, committing every detail of her features to memory. "I can't lose you,

Sacha. You have to come back to me. I'm so sorry I left you alone. I'm so sorry…"

Ricki leaned his head against the wall, resting his eyes for a moment. Jessie had been in with Sacha for a little over an hour and he wanted to be awake when he came back. He knew all too well the feeling of helplessness after someone you care about has gone through something as traumatic as this, and he needed Jessie to know that he was here for him if he ever needed to talk. It was the least he could do for him after he'd tried to help him win Maddi back.

Maddi.

She was curled into his side, one hand on his chest, the other wrapped around his back. He could tell from her steady breaths, that she had been asleep for a while now. Just that alone was enough to bring a smile to his face. She was back in his arms, resting peacefully. For now, at least.

He wasn't naïve enough to believe that everything could go back to the way it was. He knew he'd hurt her, albeit accidentally. He was so used to her being around, that he'd taken it for granted she'd always be there. What happened with Sacha tonight was a reminder that anything could happen. You can't plan for everything.

He had thought that he needed to make some grand gesture to prove how much he loved her, when really, all he ended up doing was pushing her away. He realised now that all he'd really needed to do was to be with her. Actually *be* present in the moment with her.

One thing was for sure, Ricki was prepared to do whatever it took to make her happy, for as long as she would let him.

"You're still here?" Jessie's voice came from across the room, interrupting him from his thoughts.

"Yeah, of course. I didn't think you'd want to be here alone," Ricki said quietly so as not to disturb Maddi. "Nobody should have to be on their own at a time like this."

"Thanks, man. I appreciate it." Jessie slumped down in one of the chairs opposite. He looked exhausted. His eyes were red-rimmed and bloodshot. He could barely keep them open.

"Why don't I drive you home? You can catch some sleep and then come back when you're fresh," Ricki offered.

Scrubbing his hand down his face, Jessie bobbed his head up and down in the smallest of movements. "Sleep sounds great." He glanced up with a look of guilt in his eyes. "But I shouldn't leave her. What if she wakes up?"

"Then she'll have nurses to keep her company until you're able to be back here." Before he could protest, Ricki added, "You're no good to her if you're dead on your feet." He cringed at his choice of words. "Sorry."

"I just don't want her to feel like she's been abandoned again," Jessie said in a pained voice.

"She won't, I promise. By the time she gets out of here, she'll be sick of the sight of us." Ricki grinned.

Jessie managed a laugh despite his fatigue. "I don't want to be gone long," he said, giving in.

"Okay, well I'll set my alarm, and I'll be back to pick you up around 9AM. That gives us almost five hours of sleep."

"You don't have to drive me," Jessie said through a yawn. "I have my car."

"And you will fall asleep at the wheel. We don't need another friend in the hospital, thank you very much. I'll drive, and you can take your car home later, okay?"

Nodding his head in agreement, Jessie pushed himself up to stand. "Thanks, Ricki. You're a good guy. I can see why she loves you so much." He gestured to the sleeping Maddi in his lap.

"The feeling is mutual," he said, grinning down at her.

Chapter 18

Rory shuffled down the hallway, her robe hanging loosely. She rubbed at her eyes but couldn't get rid of that scratchy feeling of tiredness. "Coffee," she muttered, moving through the kitchen on auto-pilot.

They'd spent a good chunk of Sunday at the hospital with Sacha and it had been another late night. Probably not the best thing to do the day before her first day at *Gastronomie*.

She had set her alarm nice and early so she would have plenty of time to get organised and pick the perfect outfit. This was the only chance she would get to make a first impression with her classmates, and she wanted it to be a good one.

After adding an extra scoop of coffee to her cup, she quickly inhaled the delicious aroma, allowing it to wake her up a little more. "Mmmm, coffee. How would I survive without you?"

Taking a sip, she instantly pulled the cup away, staring at it as if it were offensive. "What the?" she muttered, grabbing the milk and checking the use-by date. "Nope, still good." She turned back to her cup and tentatively brought it up to her lips. "Oh God, not again!" She slammed the cup down, sploshing the hot liquid everywhere before racing to the bathroom.

"This… can't… be… happening," she gurgled as she retched into the toilet.

She sat back, swiping a handful of toilet paper across her mouth as she tried to catch her breath. With as much effort as she could muster, she slowly pulled herself up to her feet. The basket of supplies in the corner caught her eye, and a sinking feeling hit the pit of her stomach.

"No," she whispered, counting back on her fingers. "Shit!" she hissed under her breath. "Fuck!" Tears sprang to her eyes as she began to pace back and forth. "What am I gonna do?"

"About what?" Damon asked, poking his head into the bathroom. Seeing her tear-streaked face, he quickly closed the gap between them. "What is it, babe? What's wrong?"

At a loss for words, Rory simply brought her hand to her stomach and nodded towards the toilet.

"Oh, you're still sick?" Rory bobbed her head up and down, not trusting herself to speak without breaking down further. Pulling her into his chest, he ran a soothing hand down her back. "It's okay, babe. I'm sure they'll understand that you can't make it."

Frowning, Rory stepped back. "I have to go," she said. "If I don't, I'll lose my place." Of that she was certain.

"But you can't be rushing off to the bathroom every few minutes. And what about the other students? You could make them sick too," he tried to reason.

Shaking her head firmly, Rory said, "No. I have to be there. I'll be fine. It always clears during the day, you know that."

Pressing his lips together, he didn't look convinced. "Rory…"

"I'm going, Damo. I worked too hard to get in to throw it all away on the first day." Stepping around him to the sink, she turned the cold tap on and held her hands underneath before splashing some water in her face. Bracing her hands on the edge, she looked up into the mirror, seeing the concern in his face staring back at her. Sighing, she turned back to face him. "I promise, if it doesn't go away, I'll come home, okay?" She brought her hand up to his forehead, smoothing out the crease.

"Rest as much as you can, and drink lots of water," he said, knowing there was no way he could stop her once her mind was set. "And call me if you need me to come get you."

"Aye aye, Cap'n," she said with a tired grin and a salute.

"Maddi?" Rory whispered, sneaking into her best friend's room.

"Mmmm?" a voice murmured from under the covers.

"Maddi, I need to ask you a favour." She tip-toed around the bed to Maddi's side, careful not to wake Ricki. Stroking her hair from her face in an attempt to wake her up, she tried again. "Maddi?"

One eye flickered open. "What time is it?" she mumbled. "It feels early."

Glancing at the alarm clock on the bedside table, Rory felt bad for waking her. "Um, it's 6AM."

"Rory," she whined, rolling over.

"Maddi, please. I need your help. It's important." She held her breath, waiting for Maddi to tell her to leave.

Instead, she rolled back over to face her. "Okay, what is it? This better be life-threatening."

"Um, well it's not life-threatening per se. More… life-altering." She sighed, this was harder than she thought. "I… um… I need you to get me something. I have course today, so I can't do it myself…" *Just spit it out already!* "I… um… I need," she lowered her voice even more, "a pregnancy test." She winced.

Maddi blinked, her eyes darting side-to-side. "Are you serious?" When Rory nodded her head, she reached a hand out to cup her cheek. "Really?"

"Maybe? I don't know. I've been so busy with getting into *Gastronomie* that I don't remember the last time I had my monthly, and I've been so sick lately. It's the only thing that makes sense," she said in a hushed voice, really not wanting Ricki to find out before Damon. "Maddi, I'm scared. I don't think I'm ready to be a mum, and what about Damo?" Her voice cracked as tears began to slide down her face for the second time today.

"Are you kidding? You and Damo would make great parents."

"We haven't even discussed children yet," she sobbed, burying her face in the sheets.

"Hey." Maddi lifted Rory's chin to face her. "He will be over the moon."

"You think?" she asked, wiping her eyes with the back of her hand.

"I know."

Rory smiled. "Thanks."

"Of course." Rory stood up to leave, but Maddi grabbed her hand. "Don't worry. We'll get through this."

Chapter 19

It was coming up 48 hours that Sacha had been under. They kept telling Jessie it was normal for it to take a while under such circumstances, but he couldn't help feeling that they were humouring him. He'd barely left her side, except for the few hours when Ricki had made him go home to sleep that first night. They'd all tried to convince him that she would be okay, but he didn't want her waking up without him there. Instead, he'd taken to dragging the over-stuffed chair in the corner to the side of her bed and sleeping there.

Maddi and Ricki had not long left. They'd been in to see her several times, talking to her and letting her know that they, and the whole dance community were all there for her. The large bouquet of flowers they'd brought in stood on a table to her side with a card attached, signed by the dancers.

Jessie was overwhelmed by the generosity of the community he'd grown to love over the last few years. They really were like a family. Which she was going to need when this was all over.

He'd tried on numerous occasions to get her mother to come and visit, but she flat out refused, using the excuse that she didn't like hospitals. He had heard the slurring of her words and knew she was really too wasted to give a shit. She'd never shown an interest in Sacha the entire time he'd known her, so he didn't know why he'd expected any differently this time around. Still, he gave it another shot.

"Hi, Mrs Barrett? It's Jessie. Sacha still hasn't woken up. I thought maybe you could stop by and talk to her? See if your voice might help bring her back to us?" His voice caught in his throat as he said that last part. He was so scared that she would never wake up, hence the reason for his continued perseverance with Barbara.

He held his breath, waiting for her to say something. After a long silence and a drawn-out sigh, she finally responded. "Honey, what makes you think I'm gonna come? You think if you keep callin', I'll come runnin'?"

"She's your daughter. Don't you even care what happens to her?" he asked, unable to comprehend what kind of mother could treat her daughter that way.

"She stopped bein' my daughter the minute she up an' left me high an' dry. Do me a favour. Don't call again." The phone clicked signalling the end of the call, and Jessie sat there staring at his phone in stunned silence. Sacha had told him they had a strained relationship, and that she'd left when her mother began expecting more than she was willing to give, but he'd still never imagined that she could be so cruel. He was beginning to see why Sacha was the way she was.

"Dude, you have a minute?" Damon asked, poking his head into Ricki's room.

"Sure, what's up?" Damon stepped inside, looking around the room to check that Maddi wasn't around before closing the door behind him. "You okay? You seem a little tense?" Ricki asked with a look of amusement.

"Ah, yeah. I saw something earlier today." He lowered his voice, moving closer. "Something that I think you might want to know about."

"Okay?" Ricki sat up, a frown creasing his brow. "What is it?"

"I went to go get Rory some chocolates to celebrate her first day at course, and I happened to walk past the pharmacy on the corner." He paused, taking a breath. "Maddi was in there." He looked up, concern all over his face.

"And?"

"She was looking at pregnancy tests."

Ricki went white as a ghost. "Pregnancy tests? Are you sure?"

Damon nodded. "Yeah, I'm sure. I didn't know if I should say anything or not, but I figured you had a right to know if she was, ya know," he held his hands out in front of him as if rubbing a pregnant belly. "I know I'd want to know."

Ricki sat back, raking his hand through his hair. "Wow. This… This is big. I can't believe it. I could be a father," he said under his breath. Slowly a smile spread across his face. "I could be a father," he said again.

Chapter 20

"Did you get it?" Rory practically pounced on Maddi as she walked through the door. Swivelling her head side-to-side, checking they were alone, Maddi nodded her head, retrieving a brown paper bag from her purse.

"I got two, just in case." She held the parcel out for Rory to grab. Biting her lip, Rory hesitated, almost too scared to accept it for fear it may make it real. "I can hold onto them until you're ready, if you want," Maddi offered.

"No!" Rory said, reaching for the bag. "I… I need to know." Peering inside, she sucked in a breath. "What if I do it wrong?"

Placing her hands over Rory's, Maddi smiled at her. "I'm sure they have instructions. Do you want me to read them with you? With both of us, I'm sure we'll get it right."

"Would you?"

Tilting her head to the side, Maddi shrugged. "Of course. That's what friends are for, isn't it?"

Fighting back tears for the fourth time that day, Rory simply nodded, an appreciative smile on her face. "Thanks, Maddi. For everything."

Waving her hand dismissively, she said, "Stop, I haven't done anything." She walked over to the bathroom door, her hand poised over the handle. "You wanna do it now?"

"Mmmhmm. I need to know. I spent all day worrying about it." She looked down at her hand resting on her belly and smiled. "It's funny how just the thought of a baby inside makes you start doing this."

"It just shows how great you'll be as a mother. You're already protective of the little thing." Maddi grinned, taking hold of Rory's hand and leading her through to the bathroom. "Now, let's have a look at these tests."

"And it wasn't until I went to the bathroom that I realised I had flour all through my hair!" Rory ran her hand through her short crop, sending another dusting of flour into the air. "I guess there was more floating about than I thought." She shrugged.

"All from a burst bag?"

"Yeah, well, I *did* drop it on the bench. It kinda went poof into the air." She moved her hands in arcs above her to demonstrate. "Not exactly the best start to the course."

"Hey, at least they'll remember who you are." Maddi grinned, giving her leg a playful shove.

"I'd rather they remembered me for my cooking, not my fuck-ups."

"They will, sweetie, give it time. Everyone has off days, yours just happened to be on the first day of course. Tomorrow, it'll be someone else. You'll see." Maddi paused to check her watch. "It's time," she whispered, glancing at the two sticks balanced on the edge of the vanity. They had been sitting on the bathroom floor for the past five minutes, discussing anything but the reason they were in there.

Inhaling deeply, Rory pulled her knees into her chest. "I'm scared."

"I know." Maddi scooted over to sit beside her, resting her head on her shoulder. "We can give it a few more minutes if you want."

"I want to know, but I don't at the same time, you know? Like, once I see the results, everything changes."

"Not necessarily. It could be a false alarm," Maddi offered.

"True, but…"

"But you think it's positive," Maddi finished for her.

"Yeah. I do."

"We'll get through this. No matter what the results, we'll work this out."

Puffing out a breath, Rory slapped her hands on her thighs before pushing herself up to stand. "Okay. Let's do this." She reached down to help Maddi up. Holding hands, they stepped up to the vanity and each took hold of a stick. "Two lines," Rory whispered.

“Yup. Two lines.” Maddi gave her hand a squeeze.

“I guess I’m pregnant.”

Chapter 21

"What do you think they're doing in there?" Damon asked, his arms folded across his chest as he eyed the bathroom door.

"Considering what you saw, I think it's pretty obvious, don't you?"

"I guess. It's taking them a while though."

"You ever taken a test before?" Ricki asked, one eyebrow cocked.

"No." Damon scoffed, turning his attention away from the door.

"Well, then you don't know how long it takes, do you?" Ricki made his way into the kitchen. "Coffee?" he asked, switching the jug on.

"Sure." He watched Ricki as he pulled two mugs down from the cupboard. "How can you be so calm?"

Sighing, Ricki braced his hands on the counter. "How am I supposed to be? We don't know anything yet. No point in stressing over something that may or may not happen." He shrugged, turning back to his task.

Shaking his head, Damon said, "I don't get you sometimes, man. Only a few days ago you were stressing over her not talking to you, and now that she might be," he lowered his voice, "pregnant, you look like you couldn't care less."

"Yeah well, it only takes one day to change your perspective." He ran his hand through his hair, grabbing the back of his neck. "What happened to Sacha scared the shit out of me. What if it had been Maddi? I mean, I was scared when she took off, but the thought of anything happening to her terrifies me. So, as long as she's safe and willing to have me in her life, I'm happy." Dropping his arm, he looked out the window, a grin spreading across his face. "And honestly, the thought of raising a baby with Maddi? I couldn't think of anything better."

"When you put it that way…" Damon trailed off, his eyes travelling back to the bathroom. "It would be kinda nice to have a little bundle of joy with Rory."

"We're the lucky ones, Damo." Ricki handed him his cup. "I can't imagine what Jessie is going through right now."

Damon's face dropped. "When I think about what that bastard did…" He clenched his fists by his side. "I don't care how fucked up she was, Sacha didn't deserve that."

"No, she didn't." Maddi stood in the doorway, her phone in her hand. "That was Jessie. Sacha just had another seizure."

"Jessie." Maddi ran into her friend's arms, pulling him firm against her. "Shh, she'll be okay. She'll get through this," she soothed as she ran her hands up and down his back. He clung to her as if she were the only thing holding him up, his hands grasping her shirt. With his face buried in the crook of her neck, he sobbed, his whole body shaking. "Just let it out." She continued to stroke his back and neck, trying to stay strong for him.

"She opened her eyes," he whispered when he pulled back. "She looked at me and smiled, before…" His face crumpled as fresh tears trailed their way down his cheeks. He shook his head. "I'm sorry," he whispered.

"Aww, Jessie," she said softly, cupping her hands around his face. "You have nothing to be sorry for." She gently wiped his tears from his cheeks. "Maybe she's trying to come back to us," she offered with a hesitant smile. "It could be a good sign. You just have to stay positive."

"Maybe," he whispered, but she could tell he didn't believe his own words.

Sliding her hands down his arms, she grasped his hands. "Come and sit down, you look like you've barely slept." His face was drawn, his eyes lined with a shadow that hadn't been there before.

"I haven't."

"Jessie, I know you want to be here for her, but you need to look after yourself too. You're no good to her if you fall apart." She led him to one of the couches in the corner, gently pushing on his shoulders to get him to sit. "Why don't you rest for a bit? We'll wake you if there's any news." She gestured to the others who had settled down the other end of the room.

"I don't know if I can," he said, all emotion gone from his voice.

"Please try." She sat next to him, running her fingers through his hair attempting to relax him. "Just close your eyes for a minute." She began to hum softly.

As much as he wanted to fight it, his eyes began to flutter as she kept up her gentle massage of his temples. When she was sure he was asleep, she slipped off the couch, and over to the others.

"Poor guy," Rory said with a sympathetic look. "He looks exhausted."

"Yeah. He's been staying here. I doubt he's had any sleep at all since that first night when we made him go home." Maddi wrapped her arms around herself. "I just wish there was something we could do."

"You are doing something," Ricki said, coming to stand beside her. He tipped her chin up to look at him. "You're here." Nodding, Maddi leaned into him, needing his strength. He ran his palm in soothing circles on her back, until she finally stepped away and joined the others on the couch.

A throat cleared in the doorway. "Are you here for Sacha Barrett?" the woman in scrubs asked, her hands clasped in front of her.

"Yes, we are." Maddi looked over at Jessie, wondering if she should wake him or let him sleep. "Is she okay? Can we see her now?" She made her way over to the door, her arms folded across her chest as if warding off the cold.

"I'm so sorry," she began, "the seizure caused a clot in her brain, and it travelled to her heart." She paused, her eyes flitting to the floor and back again. "I'm so sorry, there was nothing we could do."

"No," Maddi whispered, shaking her head. Ricki came up behind her, wrapping his arms around her shoulders.

"I'm afraid so. Is there anyone you'd like me to call?"

"No, her family… they're not…" She couldn't wrap her head around what the doctor had just said. *She's gone?*

"They're not around? I understand."

Maddi couldn't believe what she was hearing. Her eyes flicked to Jessie curled in the corner. "Jessie…" A sob escaped her lips. "Jessie," she said a little louder, shaking Ricki's hands from her shoulders. She walked over to the couch, gingerly perching on the edge. She reached up to touch his face. "Jessie."

"Hmmm?" he mumbled, stirring. When he saw the looks on his friends' faces, he sat upright, as if he'd forgotten where he was. "What is it? Is it Sacha?" he asked, turning to look at Maddi. "Is she okay?"

"Honey, I'm so sorry," she said, fresh trails of tears teeming down her face. "There was a blood clot… she didn't make it."

"She didn't…" he stared into her eyes, hoping that it was some sort of sick joke.

"No, I'm sorry, Jess." She shook her head, hating the pained look in his eyes. "I'm so sorry."

"She can't be gone," he said, his voice catching in his throat. "I never got to tell her how I felt. I never got to tell her I made a mistake." He closed his eyes, forcing the tears to fall. "I love her," he whispered, turning his face into Maddi's hand.

"She knew, Jess. And she loved you too," Maddi said, trying to hold it together. Sliding her hand to the back of his neck, she slowly pulled him into her arms. "She knew," she repeated, cradling him against her.

Chapter 22

The next few days flew by in a daze. Sacha's mother wasn't interested in saying goodbye, and she refused to offer any kind of help to Jessie. In the end, Maddi, Rory, and the boys had rallied around, helping him to organise the funeral and wake.

Maddi and Rory stood by the door, handing out memorial cards to all the people who had come to celebrate the life of Sacha. The salsa community had come out in full force, filling the room with their vibrant colours, rather than the traditional black; something Sacha would have done had she still been here. The sound of cow bells could be heard from out on the street as some of her favourite salsa songs were played.

"I still can't believe she's gone," Nicole said softly as she pulled Maddi in for a hug.

"I know. I keep expecting her to barge through that door and tell us all to harden up." Maddi smiled, though it didn't quite reach her eyes. "Is Rob with the boys?"

"Yeah, they shouldn't be too far away. They were almost ready to head over when I left."

"How'd Jessie look?" Maddi's face was lined with worry. Despite her encouragement, she knew he'd barely eaten or slept since the attack. Not that she could blame him; it hadn't been easy for any of them.

"Not good to be honest. He looks dead on his feet." She gasped, her hand covering her mouth. "Sorry, that was in bad taste. It just slipped out."

Maddi dismissed the comment with a wave of her hand. "Don't worry about it." As she watched Nicole make her way into the hall, the hairs on the back of her neck stood on end and she knew without looking, that they had arrived.

Swallowing back the lump in her throat, she placed the leftover cards on the table and, taking Rory's hand, she walked down the steps to join her friends by the hearse.

"Jessie," she whispered, reaching out and wrapping her arms around him. She rubbed her hands up and down his back, fighting back the urge to cry. When she pulled away, she could see the glisten in his eyes and offered a sympathetic smile. "You ready?"

With a longing look at the coffin, he nodded. "Yes."

Jessie and Ricki each took hold of the front, Maddi and Rory stood in the middle, clasping the cool metal handles, while Rob and Damon took hold of the rear.

"On the count of three. One, two, three." They lifted the mahogany box from its holder, and with slow steps, they made their way across the lot and entered the hall.

One by one, the guests stood, a silence falling around the room as the soulful voice of Garth Brooks singing "The Dance" played over the speakers. Once at the front, Maddi placed a picture of Sacha on top of the box, a white rose beside it. They each held their palms to the wood in a final goodbye before taking their seats.

"Please be seated. On behalf of Jessie, I would like to thank you all for coming to celebrate the life of Sacha Barrett. A life taken far too soon." The celebrant paused, looking out across the room. "It is heart-warming to see so many friends here, not only to say goodbye to such a charismatic woman, but to support Jessie in this difficult time. He will continue to need your love and support over the coming weeks."

Jessie nodded his head, his eyes fixed on the photos flashing on the screen behind the celebrant. The photos of him and Sacha. Hot tears slowly trickled down his cheeks as he remembered each and every moment spent with her.

"As many of you know, Sacha was well known in the Latin dance community, and Rachel would like to say a few words on their behalf."

The redhead walked down the aisle and took her place at the podium. "Hi. For those of you who don't know me, I'm one of the dance teachers in this community. I was lucky enough to teach Sacha and Jessie." She looked over to where Jessie sat, her voice faltering. "Right from the beginning, I knew she was going to be something special. She had this fire inside that wanted to come out. You could see it every time she danced." She shook her head with a smile. "She certainly had the fiery attitude to go with it. No one could ever say she didn't put her all into everything she did. She had a lot of potential, and I wish she could have had more time to show the world." Looking down at the casket, she said, "We're going to miss you, Sacha. I hope you're still dancing up there, showing them how it's done." She stepped down and made her way over to Jessie, placing her hand on his shoulder. Looking up at her, he patted her hand and thanked her for her kind words.

"Thank you for that, Rachel. I'm sure she will be dancing up a storm." The celebrant smiled. "Maddi, would you like to come to the front?"

Maddi nodded, taking hold of Jessie's hand as they stepped up to the podium together. Clearing her throat, she began. "Jessie has written a few words down and asked me to read them out." She reached back for his hand, giving it a squeeze. "Sacha, you took my breath away from the first moment I saw you dance. And even though you were with a friend of mine at the time, I couldn't help but be drawn to you and your stubborn, strong-willed fierceness." She smiled at his choice of words; Sacha definitely was all of those. "We had our ups and downs, but no matter what, I never stopped loving you. I only wish I could have told you that one more time." She paused, taking a breath as she felt the tears brimming.

"To everyone around us, you put on a show, never letting them see your softer side, but with me, there was no hiding. I was lucky enough to have a glimpse into your vulnerability, your kindness, and your dreams. I wish we'd had the time to show the world what you were really capable of. You were my friend, my mentor, and my lover. I love you more than words can say. I'd give anything to be able to hold you one last time." Unable to stop the tears, she brought her hand to her face, brushing them away. "Sorry," she said, trying to compose herself.

With a shaking voice, she managed to get out the last few words. "Sacha, I hope you know how much you mean to me. I will always hold you in my heart. Keep on dancing, wherever you are. Love you, babe."

Turning to face Jessie, she flung her arms around him as they both fell apart, crying over the woman who had driven them both crazy.

Chapter 23

Carrying Sacha back to the hearse and watching Jessie say his final goodbye had been one of the hardest things Maddi had ever had to do. She couldn't begin to imagine how he must've been feeling, knowing that Sacha would never be in his arms again.

One by one, people began to move forward, offering their condolences. Jessie stood rigidly, his hands clasped in front of him and a vacant stare in his eyes, his body moving on autopilot whenever someone pulled him in for a hug.

With Maddi and Ricki on either side of him, he slowly made his way up the steps and back into the warmth of the reception hall. Rory and the other students from *Gastronomie* had transformed the room in a matter of minutes. Long trestle tables were draped with bright cloths, and a myriad of nibbles were scattered across each table. To the side of the room was a drinks bar, complete with fancy barista-style coffee and flavoured teas.

When Rory saw them step into the room, she quickly strode over, her black apron strings streaming out behind her. "Can I get you something to drink? Coffee? Tea?"

"Um, no. Thanks though. You've done a wonderful job in here, Rory." His voice cracked and his eyes flew to the ceiling as he composed himself.

"Jessie, you need to have something. How about a sweet tea to warm you up?" Maddi nodded to Rory, and she scurried away to get it before he could protest.

"I'm fine, Maddi."

"I know you are. Humour me, okay? Let us take care of you in the way we know how."

The tiniest hint of a smile appeared on his face, and Maddi finally felt like she was getting somewhere with him.

"Believe me, it's easier to just let her have her way," Ricki said out of the side of his mouth.

"Hey! I heard that." Maddi slapped him playfully on the arm. "He's right though," she said with a wink.

Jessie turned to her with an exaggerated sigh. "If it will get you to stop pestering me, I'll drink the tea."

"Good, and it will… after you eat something as well." She grinned up at him, batting her lashes. "Please? Just something small."

"Oh all right then."

Maddi clapped her hands together before making her way to the food. Grabbing a small plate, she carefully selected a ham, egg and mayo sandwich, a piece of red velvet cake, and some chocolate fudge.

"Here you go," she said as she thrust the plate towards him.

"Something small, eh?" He raised an eyebrow as he took the plate from her hands.

"Just giving you choices. How's your tea?"

"It's good. Thank you." He smiled, the first genuine smile she'd seen from him since Sacha's passing. "And thank you for organising all of this." His eyes travelled the room. "It's perfect."

Placing her hand on his forearm, Maddi nodded her head. "It was our pleasure."

"I know things weren't great between you two, and for you to go to all this trouble for her… It would mean a lot to her."

"I'm just doing what anyone else would do."

"No, I don't think anyone else *would* do this. You're a good person, Maddi. And for what it's worth, she had a lot of respect for you, she just didn't know how to show it. Most people would bend over backwards to keep her happy, but you challenged her. You pushed her to be her best, even if it didn't seem that way to anyone else."

Maddi's eyes brimmed with tears as her thoughts turned to all the times she'd gone up against Sacha. "I wish I'd tried harder to get to know her better."

Jessie shrugged. "It takes two to tango. She was just as stubborn as you, if not more." He stared into his cup of tea, swirling the liquid around. "I'm really going to miss her."

"I know. I think we all will."

Jessie scoffed, raising his eyes to meet hers. "You don't have to say that."

"No, really. All competitiveness aside, she was an amazing dancer. She brought a fire to the dancefloor that not many possess."

Nodding his head, Jessie agreed. "You're right, she did."

"And let's face it, there was never a dull moment when she was around." Maddi nudged him with her elbow.

A slow smile spread across his face. "Yeah, she was a firecracker."

"She certainly was," a voice came from behind Maddi, making the hairs on the back of her neck stand on end.

"Dane, I didn't expect to see you here." Jessie held his hand out to his old friend. "It's been a long time."

Maddi stood frozen to the spot, her heart pounding in her chest as they continued talking beside her as if her world weren't crashing around her ears.

"I wasn't sure if I should come, but I wanted to pay my respects." Dane shoved his hands in his pockets, his eyes flicking over to Maddi.

"Of course you should be here, you were a huge part of her life too." Jessie raked his hand through his hair. "Sorry, I should've called and told you."

"Hey, don't stress about it. You had other things on your mind. It's understandable." Turning his eyes to Maddi, who still hadn't moved, he reached out to touch her arm. "Maddi?" he said softly when she shrugged away from his touch. "It's good to see you. You look good."

The slight brush of his fingers on her skin had her wanting to scream. Her eyes filled with unshed tears and her breath came out in sharp pants. She couldn't be here with him. She needed to get away, but no matter how hard she tried, her legs wouldn't obey her. She was paralysed with fear, her brain unable to cooperate with her body.

"Maddi, are you okay?" Jessie moved to stand in front of her, a look of concern on his face.

"Oh hell no!" A crash across the room drew his attention as Rory stormed towards them, her nostrils flaring and her finger pointed at Dane.

In a flash, Damon grabbed her around the waist, her arms and legs flailing as she tried to get out of his grasp. "Not here," he hissed in her ear. "Not now."

"Maddi?" Ricki moved to stand beside her, coaxing her into his arms, shielding her from the man who forced himself on her. "Come on, let's go outside and get some air." Pinning Dane with his eyes over her shoulder, he mouthed the words, *Stay away from her.*

Dane held his hands up, palms out; trying to convey his acquiescence. "Perhaps I should go, I don't want any trouble."

"I don't understand. What's going on? Is it because of the break-up?" Jessie stood between them, confused. "Maddi?"

With a shake of her head, she buried her face in Ricki's chest, clutching onto him.

"It's complicated," he said, ushering her towards the door.

"Don't leave. I'm sorry, I shouldn't have come. I thought…" He broke off, shaking his head. "Never mind. You guys stay, I'll go." Dane skirted around them, one final nod at Jessie. "I'm sorry for your loss."

Chapter 24

"He had no right to be there!" Rory paced back and forth in the lounge, her hands on her hips. "I mean, what did he think was going to happen? She'd welcome him back with open arms?"

"Easy, tiger." Damon took hold of her shoulders, making her stop and look at him. "It was a funeral, and he used to date her. It makes sense that he'd want to say his goodbyes."

"Yeah, but he could've done that from afar. He didn't need to come anywhere near her." Her eyes flicked down the hall to where Maddi was. "Did you see the look on her face? She was terrified."

"Yeah, I saw." His fists clenched at his sides. "Believe me, I wanted to deck him just as much as you did, but a funeral is not the place to be doing it."

With an exaggerated sigh, Rory threw herself onto the couch. "I know, you're right. I wasn't thinking straight. When I saw him reaching out to her…ugh! I just wanted to…" She mimed ripping something apart with her bare hands. "You know?"

"Yeah, I know. He'll get his, don't you worry. Karma has a way of catching up on people like that."

"It bloody well better." Folding her arms across her chest, she stared off down the hall again. "What do you think they're doing in there?"

"She'll be fine. Stop worrying. Ricki's got this." Offering his hands out to her, he nodded his head towards the kitchen. "Come on, let's get some of those leftovers packaged up for Jessie. I doubt he feels much like cooking."

"You're a real softy sometimes, you know that?" Taking his hands, she allowed him to pull her off the couch.

"Don't act so surprised. You know that's why you love me so much." He winked, leading her into the kitchen. "Seriously though, it's put things into perspective." Turning to rest his hip against the counter, he pulled her into his arms, resting his chin on her head. "I would be a mess if anything ever happened to you. I feel really sorry for the guy."

Squeezing her arms that little bit tighter around his middle, she nodded against his chest. "Yeah, it's pretty scary how quickly things can change." Tucking her head down, she stared at the flat expanse of her stomach, picturing how it would look in a few more months. She knew he had a right to know that he was going to be a father, but the timing felt all wrong. How could they celebrate when Jessie's life was crumbling around him? It didn't seem fair.

Not to mention Dane being back on the scene threw a spanner in the works. It hardly felt like the time to drop the baby bomb on everyone. She still had to figure out what she was going to do about *Gastronomie*. For the past few years it was all she'd dreamed of, and she'd be damned if it was going to be taken away from her. There had to be a way to have both.

"Hey, guys," Maddi said from the doorway, her fingers tangling together. "I'm sorry about before. I kinda freaked out a bit."

"*You* freaked out?" Rory stepped around Damon to give her friend a hug. "Please. I was the one who smashed a plate and had to be hauled out of there. If anyone is going to be apologising for freaking out, it's me."

Maddi chuckled lightly. "You smashed a plate?"

"Oh yeah, like full-on judo chop!" She pulled back, displaying some over-dramatic karate moves, complete with sound effects. "I would've gone all Daniel-san on his ass if Damo hadn't stepped in."

"Believe me, it was tempting to let you go all *Crouching Tiger* on him, but I didn't think Jessie would appreciate the sentiment." Damon chuckled as he began shovelling various slices into containers. "It would have made for a great show though."

"I'd pay to see it," Ricki said, giving Rory a high five on his way passed. "He deserves all that and more."

"Oh yeah. And I'm happy to be the one who dishes it out."

Ricki grinned. "I think we all would, Rory. Though, I think you'd be quite the worthy adversary." He held his hands in front of him, palms facing each other. "Compact. And quick."

"Mmhmm," Damon agreed. "You've gotta protect the twig and berries from this one, she's sneaky and just the right height to surprise punch 'em."

"That was one time, and I said I was sorry." Rory pouted. "I only meant to tap them." She shrugged her shoulders. "Apparently I don't know my own strength."

"Just a tap," Damon muttered under his breath. "Damn near had me on my knees with tears in my eyes."

"Oh, stop! It wasn't that bad!"

"Wasn't it? I may never be able to have children," he said mockingly while he flapped his hand in front of his face like a damsel in distress.

Rory's face dropped. How wrong he was.

Knowing exactly what her friend was thinking, Maddi took hold of her hand and gave a squeeze before joining the boys in the kitchen. "Let's get all this food sorted out so we can take it to Jessie."

Chapter 25

"Thanks for letting me stop by. I probably should've done this from the start instead of causing a scene back there." Dane hooked his thumb over his shoulder as he rocked on his heels in the doorway.

"No problem. It's good to see you again. Come in, have a coffee." Jessie stepped back from the door, allowing room for him to pass.

"That would be nice, thanks." As Dane followed Jessie down the hall, he took in the barren walls and boxes filling the open space.

"Sorry about the mess. I only just moved in here when…" He cleared his throat before continuing. "I've only been here a little while." Averting his eyes, he made a beeline for the kitchen, switching the kettle on, while Dane wandered around the room aimlessly.

"Where's all her things?" he asked quietly.

With his hands gripping the counter, Jessie took a shaking breath. "Still at the old place," he whispered. "We'd… we were having a break…"

"Oh sorry, I didn't realise. I just assumed…" Dane trailed off, silently kicking himself for sticking his nose in where it wasn't needed. "It's a nice place," he said, desperately trying to appease the situation.

"It's all right. Does the job." He shrugged then set to work on their drinks, if only to distract himself. It didn't work though, instead sending a jumble of thoughts through his mind about Sacha. Here was Dane offering an olive branch, when really it should be the other way around. He was the one who'd done Dane wrong and broken the number one rule: bros before hoes.

"I, ah… I don't think I ever apologised for what Sacha and I did to you," Jessie said as he carried their coffees through to the dining table. "I honestly never meant for any of that to happen… I don't know what came over me that day. I never thought I'd be 'that guy' but then Sacha… she could be real persuasive when she wanted to, and to be honest, I don't think I tried hard enough to stay away. She was…" he breathed out a sigh. "God, she was something else."

"Don't I know it?" With a shake of his head, he continued. "You don't have to apologise. It's water under the bridge now." Dane clasped his hands together. "I mean, if that hadn't happened, I never would have found Maddi." He took a sip of his coffee.

"That didn't exactly go well either though, did it? I'm not sure I did you any kind of favour." Jessie leaned forward. "If you don't mind me asking, what happened between you two? I thought it was mutual, but after what I saw today…"

Dane ran his fingers through his hair. "I'd rather not talk about it. Let's just say, it wasn't my finest moment." He gazed out the window, his fingers gently drumming on his cup. "I didn't mean to upset her, you know. I only wanted to clear the air."

Jessie eyed him wearily. "Whatever went down between you two is your business I guess, and I'm sure when she's ready to, she'll hear you out." He paused, leaning back on his chair. "You know, she was probably just surprised to see you again. What's it been? Eighteen months? That's a long time."

"Mmmm." Dane nodded. "It really is."

"Do you think you'll come back to dancing?"

"I'd like to, but…" He turned to look at Jessie. "I don't want to make Maddi uncomfortable. This is her domain now."

"There's other studios, you don't have to dance at hers." Jessie shrugged. "Maybe it's time to branch out?"

"Yeah, maybe." Pushing his chair back, Dane stood up, bracing his hands against the table. "I should let you get back to it. It was really good seeing you again." He smiled though Jessie could see the hurt in his eyes.

"Yeah, you too. And I'm sorry I didn't call… I…there's really no excuse for it. I was just lost."

"I understand. I would've been the same way." His voice caught in his throat. "I still can't believe she's really gone. I thought she'd outlive all of us." He laughed without mirth.

"If only that were true." Jessie shoved his hands in his pockets, staring at his feet. "Goes to show, nothing in life is guaranteed. It only takes the act of some arsehole to ruin everything."

Swallowing the lump in his throat, Dane could only nod, unable to think of anything to say. How could he, when he was no better than the scum who attacked Sacha? Bile roiled in his stomach as he thought about what he almost did to Maddi, what could have been if Ricki hadn't busted the door down and pulled him off her.

He'd come back to town, not only to say his goodbyes to Sacha and make amends with Jessie, but also to ask for Maddi's forgiveness. But now that he was here and listening to Jessie talk, he realised something.

He didn't deserve her forgiveness.

Chapter 26

"Are you fucking kidding me right now?" Rory roared as they rounded the corner and came face to face with Dane. Dropping the bags of food to the ground, she automatically took up a defensive stance in front of Maddi, her fists balled by her sides as she stared him down with nostrils flaring. "Why are you back?" she demanded, pointing one finger through the air.

Taking a step back with his hands up, Dane stuttered, "I-I don't want any trouble. I only came to see Jessie." He couldn't stop his eyes from straying over Rory's head to meet Maddi's. "I never meant to upset—"

"You don't get to address her," Rory interrupted. "You've put her through enough already, don't you think?"

Averting his eyes, Dane shoved his hands in his pockets, kicking a toe into the ground. "I'm sorry," he whispered. "You're right. I just..." He looked up apologetically. "I just want her to know how sorry I am... for what I did... I never should have done that." Tears brimmed his eyes as he pleaded. "I really did love her..."

Rory scoffed, putting her hands on her hips. "You've got a funny way of showing it."

"I know. I screwed up and lost the best thing that ever happened to me. Don't you think I know that already?" With a sigh and a shake of his head, Dane tried to calm down before he made matters worse. Closing his eyes, he counted backwards from ten until his breathing evened out, just like he'd been taught. "I wish I could say or do something to prove to you how truly sorry I am." Taking a chance, he peered at Maddi once more, who was watching him with a mixture of fear and understanding. "You really were the best thing to ever happen to me, and I wish to God I'd seen it sooner. Maybe things wouldn't have played out the way they did… You deserve happiness, Maddi. I hope Ricki makes you happy." After a beat, he turned on his heels and began walking away.

"Can you believe that guy?" Rory asked, hooking a thumb over her shoulder as she swivelled on the spot to retrieve the bags.

"Dane, wait!" Maddi called out, hesitantly stepping forward.

"What are you doing?" Rory watched as she took another shaky step towards him.

Dane stood with his back to them, unsure what to do. He didn't want to scare her again, not when this was the first time she'd spoken to him in over a year.

"A-are you o-okay?" she asked, stopping a safe distance behind him. They had been happy once, and even with everything he'd put her through, she still couldn't get herself to hate him. Fear him, yes, but not hate.

Nodding his head, he slowly spun to face her, keeping his hands securely in his pockets so as not to frighten her. "I am. I'm seeing things much clearer now. After… you know… I started seeing a counsellor." Pulling his hand up to his face, he rubbed his jaw. "I've been diagnosed with borderline personality disorder. Not that it's any excuse for what I did. It's never okay, and it kills me that I was able to do that to you, Maddi." He reached his hand out to her, forgetting how fragile she was. When he saw her flinch, he dropped his hand to his side. "I hate that I've hurt you. That you can't bear to be near me. I'd give anything to take it all back."

"I know," she whispered as a silent tear rolled down her cheek. She looked away, straightening her top and clearing her throat. "I hate it too, but it *did* happen, and we can't change that. All we can do is move forward, right?"

"Maddi?" Rory took her hand, offering what little support she could.

"I'm okay." She smiled through her tears. "I don't know if I'm ready to forgive you yet, Dane, but I'm going to try. It's going to take some time though."

Letting out the breath he'd been holding, Dane gave a nod of his head. "Thank you, I understand," he stammered. "You have no idea what this means to me."

"I'm not just doing it for you, I'm doing it for me too. It hurts in here." She pointed to her chest. "Every time I see you, I'm reminded of that night, and it hurts like it did back then." She shook her head of the images. "I don't want it to hurt anymore. And I don't want you to hurt either." She gestured between herself and Dane. "We can never go back to what we once were, but I'd like to try to put this behind us and maybe, one day, we could be friends again."

"Maddi, are you sure about this?" Rory asked.

"I am," she said with finality. "If Sacha's death has taught me anything, it's that everything can change in an instant, and I don't want to waste my life holding onto negative feelings. We can't change the past, but we *can* change how we feel about it." Turning back to Dane, she said, "I can see the regret in your eyes. I can feel the sorrow inside you. I knew something wasn't right back then and I should've been more receptive instead of pushing you away."

Shaking his head, Dane disagreed. "No, Maddi, don't take the blame for it. It's all on me. All of it. I didn't have a hold of my emotions back then. I was overwhelmed, and I put you in danger. I've accepted that now, and I have strategies in place so that it never happens again."

"You're damn right it won't happen again," Rory said vehemently. "Because if it did, I would hunt you down and castrate you myself." She held her fingers in the air, making a cutting motion. "Snip, snip."

"And I would willingly let you do that. I don't ever want to be that person again. You have my word, Rory, I won't hurt her again. I promise."

"Yeah, well, just know that I'll be keeping my eye on you." She pointed two fingers at her own eyes, before swinging them around to point at his. "Eye. On. You."

"I would believe that too," he said with an uncomfortable chuckle. "Anyway." He rocked back on his heels, bringing his hands together in front of him. "I don't want to hold you ladies up any longer." Side-stepping around Maddi, he gave her a smile reminiscent of their earlier days. "Thank you for hearing me out."

She watched as he walked away, the heavy burden of holding onto that hate lifting from her shoulders with each step.

Closing her eyes, she held her hand to her chest, sighing. "I can breathe again."

"At least someone can. You could warn a girl before you go all philosophical and lovey dovey."

"I'm sorry, I know you wanted to go all mini mafia on him, but it just felt like the right thing to do. Couldn't you see the pain in his eyes?"

"I mean, I guess…"

"And I love that you jump to my defence, but are you forgetting that you have someone else to think of now?" She nodded towards Rory's stomach. "That little bean doesn't need to be in a fight before he's even born."

Placing her hands on her belly, she grinned. "You think it's a boy?"

Shrugging her shoulder, Maddi gathered the bags from the ground. "I don't know, maybe."

"I kind of think it's a boy too. I keep having dreams about a blue-eyed boy with olive skin just like his daddy."

They strolled down the street in silence, counting the houses as they went by. When they reached Jessie's mailbox, Maddi stopped and faced Rory. "You know, you're going to need to tell him. He has a right to know."

"I know. It just hasn't felt like the right time, you know? With Sacha… and then Dane showing up…"

"It's as good a time as any if you ask me. People need something good to hold on to in times like this. Give him something to look forward to." Maddi walked down the path and up the steps to the door. Glancing over her shoulder, she could see Rory was rooted to the spot. "That's my view on it anyway. It's just an opinion. I mean, I'd understand if you were scared to—"

"I'm not scared." She shook her head, dragging her feet up to meet Maddi. The look of sympathy on her face made her cry out in frustration. "I'm not!"

"Okay, whatever." Maddi grinned, knowing her words would eventually grate on her friend's mind until she had to do something about it.

"I'm going to tell him when it feels right."

"Mmhmm."

With a dramatic sigh and roll of her eyes, she threw her spare arm in the air. "Fine! I'll do it tonight."

Chapter 27

"Do you think… I can't believe I'm about to say this but, do you think maybe I'm not meant to ask her to marry me?" Ricki leaned his back against the counter next to Damon.

"Not meant to ask her? Like the universe is giving you signs or something?" he retorted with a smirk.

"I knew you'd turn it into a joke. Don't worry, I shouldn't have said anything." Sighing, he pushed off from the counter. "I'm gonna go for a walk."

Before he could get out the door, Damon stopped him with a hand to his chest. "Dude, I'm sorry, I didn't realise it was that serious. You okay?"

"Yes… no… I don't know. It just feels like every time I get close to proposing, something else crops up." Clasping his hands behind his neck, he looked up to the ceiling. "Shit, I sound like an arsehole."

"Well…" Damon grinned at him with a raised eyebrow. "Maybe a little bit." He held his finger and thumb in the air with a small gap between them before clamping his hand on Ricki's shoulder. "You're allowed to think of yourself once in a while. It's not against the law."

"No, but it's insensitive. We just buried Jessie's girl, and all I can think about is how I want Maddi to be my wife."

"Funerals affect everyone in different ways. There's no right or wrong. I can totally get why it would make you think that way." He made a show of looking around to make sure they were alone, even though he knew the girls had not long left. "Has she mentioned the pregnancy test yet?"

He shook his head. "No. But I saw the stick in the trash the next day." He lifted his eyes to meet Damon's. "It was positive. I'm going to be a dad." A small smile played across his lips at the thought.

"Even more reason to pop the question, don't you think?"

"It's all I've wanted to do for the last few months, but with everything going on, it feels like maybe it's not meant to be."

"Sounds like you're taking an easy out to me." Damon folded his arms across his chest. "You nearly lost her. Twice. Man, she is the best thing that ever happened to you, and you know it. Why are you making excuses? What are you afraid of?"

"I don't know—"

"I call bullshit," he interrupted with narrowed eyes. "This is because of Dane, isn't it?"

Knowing he wouldn't let it go, Ricki decided to lay it all out. "Maybe it is." Balling his hands into fists by his side, he began to pace. "He just shows up like what he did wasn't a big deal. Like he didn't nearly destroy her." Raking his hand through his hair, he turned back to Damon. "We were making progress, she was coming back to me, and then he shows up and crushes her all over again."

"Then be the man who puts her back together. Don't back off when she needs you the most. Show her what she means to you, what *they* mean to you." He holds his hand in front of his stomach. "Man up and show her you'll be there for her, no matter what."

"It's not that simple."

"It *is* that simple. You love her, don't you?"

"Of course I do."

"You want her to have your baby, don't you?"

"You know I do."

"Then what's the problem?"

"Why hasn't she told me yet?" he whispered. "If she wanted me to be a part of their lives, why wouldn't she tell me?" The hurt in his voice was undeniable. "She's the first person I want to tell when anything good happens in my life. I thought… What if she hasn't told me because it *isn't* a good thing in her eyes? What if she doesn't want to have my baby?"

"And what if she's just scared? Have you thought about that?" Damon perched on the arm of the chair, bracing his hands on his knees. "Cut her some slack, man." He counted on his fingers. "She thought you were cheating on her, she's worried about Jessie, and now her stalker ex-boyfriend shows up out of the blue. She's had a lot to process this past week."

Sighing, Ricki nodded. "You're right. She *has* had a lot to process."

"Just be there for her. I'm sure she'll tell you when she's ready." Slapping his hands on his thighs, he stood up. "Right, now that we're done talking about our feelings," he batted his eyelashes and tilted his head to the side, "I'm gonna make a sandwich out of those leftovers. You want one?"

Chapter 28

"How're you doing?" Maddi asked as she stepped into Jessie's kitchen, making herself at home.

"As good as can be expected." He followed her in, watching her unload the containers into his fridge. "Thanks for bringing those around. I don't think I could face cooking today."

"We thought that might be the case." Rory hoisted the remaining bag up onto the bench. "I hope you like slices and sandwiches, you'll be eating them for days." She smiled, giving his arm a squeeze. "In fact, have you eaten? I can rustle a plate up for you now, if you like."

"Thanks, but I'm okay at the moment. You guys have already done so much. I can't thank you enough for all the help over the last few days."

"Oh psshh." She waved her hand dismissively. "It was the least we could do."

"Exactly. We're happy to help." Maddi handed her empty bag to him. "Pass that lot over, would you?"

"You don't have to do that. I can put them away later."

"I know you can, but like I said earlier, food is our way of helping, so just let us do it." She grinned, taking the bag from Rory's hands. "And don't think we won't be coming around to check on you. You're stuck with us I'm afraid."

"Two beautiful girls checking up on me, however will I cope?" he deadpanned with a shake of his head. "I really do appreciate it."

"We know." Maddi pushed the fridge door closed. "Right, is there anything else you need done?"

"Seriously, stop fussing. I'd rather we just hang out. It's amazing how quiet a place can get." He gazed out the window with a faraway look.

"We can do that," Maddi said, taking his hand and pressing a kiss to his cheek. "Whatever you want."

"Why don't you come back to our place? We could grab some takeout and watch a movie," Rory offered. "I'll even let you pick the movie." She said it as though it was a huge privilege she was bestowing upon him.

"I *could* use the company…"

"Then it's settled." She looped her arm through his, nudging Maddi out of the way. "We'll swing by the DVD store on the way home. What's your fancy?"

With a firm grip, she led him towards the door but not before Maddi could whisper in her ear. "You don't fool me. I know what you're doing."

"I'm inviting our friend over to spend some quality time with us. That's what I'm doing." Pretending to mull it over, she gasped. "Oh! You mean the thing I was going to disclose tonight? Oh well, I guess it'll just have to wait. What a bummer."

Her voice dripped with sarcasm as she shrugged her shoulders nonchalantly.

"If you've already got plans—"

"Nope, no plans. Free as a bird." Rory practically pushed him out the door.

"Should I even ask?" Jessie raised an eyebrow at Maddi who couldn't help but chuckle.

"Probably not. It's easier if you just run with it."

"That has got to be one of my favourite movies! Melissa McCarthy is a badarse!" Rory jumped to her feet, executing her version of the fight scene they'd just watched in *Spy*. "I could totally be an agent."

"You'd nail it, babe." Damon chuckled, grabbing hold of her hips and pulling her down onto his lap. "I could see you all in leathers, roundhouse kicking some evil mastermind."

"You could?"

"Oh yeah, in fact, maybe we could play that out later on." He nuzzled her neck, sending her into a fit of giggles.

"Ignore them. We do," Ricki said as he reached for the remote to drown out their smooching.

With a sad smile, Jessie found himself mesmerised by them. It hadn't been so long ago that he and Sacha had been the ones canoodling through a movie. What he wouldn't give to go back to one of those nights, snuggled up on the couch with her in his arms.

"You okay?" Maddi asked, noticing the wistful look in his eyes.

Forcing himself to look away, he offered her a weak smile. "Yeah, I'm okay. Just missing her is all."

"Aw, honey." Wrapping her arm around his neck, she gently pulled him in for a hug. "We'll get through this."

"I know. It feels weird to be sitting here as if nothing's happened, you know?" Slipping out of her grasp, he rested his head on the back of the couch. "I keep thinking she'll walk through that door any minute now."

"I know what you mean. It's hard to get used to the idea of not seeing her." Turning her attention back to the screen, she chewed her lip, unsure whether to say what was on her mind. He had to be getting sick of hearing everyone's opinions on how he should handle things. With a quick glance out the corner of her eye, she could see how restless he was. Deciding to speak up, she nudged him gently with her elbow. "You're allowed to enjoy a movie with friends. It doesn't have to mean anything. No one's… judging you."

"Nothing gets past you, does it?" he mumbled under his breath.

"Not when my friends are involved." She gave his knee a pat. "I know you probably feel like you're betraying her by enjoying yourself, but you're not. It's okay to try and find some peace, even if only for a moment."

Nodding his head slowly, Jessie mulled it over. What she said made sense, he knew that, but putting it into action wasn't easy. Every time he felt himself relax, her face would hover in his mind's eye and guilt would override everything. Perhaps, over time, it would get easier, but right now, he wasn't ready to let go of those feelings.

"We're all here for you, Jessie. In whatever way you need us, we're here." Her hand found his, squeezing ever so softly, a silent promise of support.

The movie all but forgotten, Jessie looked around the group surrounding him, thanking his lucky stars he still had them in his life.

Chapter 29

"Okay everyone!" Maddi clapped her hands, ushering the couples to come in closer. "I know things have been a little disjointed lately, but the comps are coming up fast and we really need to knuckle down and perfect our routine." She paused, looking to Ricki for his nod of approval. "We wanted to run something by you before we get started. As you know, the community has been dealt a hard blow with Sacha's passing, and we thought that maybe, with your permission, we could dedicate our dance to Sacha and Jessie. Sort of a homage to her passion for the dance. Maybe throw in a few of her signature moves?" She held her hand up to stop anyone from jumping in. "I know it's late in the game to be changing things up, but it just feels like the right thing to do. So, what do you think?"

"Yeah, of course. It sounds like a great idea. You know she would've been up there competing against us if she was still here. It's only fair that a bit of her comes with us," Nicole said, stepping forward. "I'm happy to do extra training sessions to get it right. I'd planned on stepping it up a notch anyways."

"It goes without saying that I'm in if she's in." Rob grinned, taking her hand and kissing her palm.

"Thanks, guys. I know Jessie will appreciate the sentiment, and you can bet your arse, Sacha will be watching us from above." Maddi grinned, turning her eyes skyward.

"No doubt about it," Ricki added.

"What I had in mind was a slight change to the intro, and in the centre shine piece, we'll incorporate some of the moves she was known for, without taking away from our original piece. Sound good?" When they'd all nodded their agreement, she continued. "This is what we've come up with so far, but feel free to throw some ideas out there. We want to make this into something spectacular."

Ricki took his place beside her and, pulling the remote from his pocket, pressed play. The haunting voice of Sarah McLachlan singing *Angels* filled the room as Maddi began to step slowly around Ricki, her hand rolling across his body until it fell into his grasp. Pulling her into him, he lowered her into a slow dip, bringing her body back up in an arc, before they moved through a series of steps Sacha had once favoured, finishing on a gentle lift. It was only a brief intro, but it was moving.

"That was beautiful," Nicole said, wiping a finger under her eyes before any tears could slip out. "Beautiful and powerful. Just like Sacha was."

Ricki placed Maddi back onto her feet. "I'm so glad you think so. It's what we were going for."

"Well, you nailed it. You want to walk us through it again?"

"Sure. Everyone take your places and we'll break it down for you."

"Okay, how does this taste?" Rory held a wooden spoon out, her other hand cupped underneath to catch any drops.

Leaning forward, Damon opened his mouth, allowing her to feed him. The heat of the chilli hit him instantly, setting his mouth on fire. He quickly grabbed for a glass, filling it with water before gulping it down.

"Damn it, too hot?" She frowned, giving the pot another stir. "I thought I'd balanced it right this time."

Flapping his hand in front of his mouth, he huffed out a few quick breaths. "I mean, it's good, it's just blow-your-head-off good. So, if that's what you were going for, then you hit the nail on the head." A light sheen of sweat had formed on his top lip and his eyes were watering. "Do we have any milk? Milk's good for spicy food, isn't it?" He didn't wait for a response, pouring himself another full glass and downing it.

"Gah! I've made chilli a thousand times before, why can't I get it right now?" She stomped over to the cupboards, wrenching the door open to see if she could find anything that would cut through the heat. "I just wanted to make a nice meal for everyone to share, and now it's ruined!" She sniffled, hating that her automatic response to anything lately was to cry.

"Babe, it's not ruined." Damon stood behind her, his large hands kneading her shoulders. "I'm sure you can come up with something amazing to go with it. And you know I'm going to end up slapping it between two slices of bread anyway."

Rory scrunched her nose. "Philistine. You're just as bad as those people who put tomato sauce on everything."

"Don't knock it till you try it. Chilli sandwiches are the shit." She tilted her head back to frown at him, and he pressed a kiss to smooth out the lines. "You know what else? My tongue is going numb, so I probably won't even notice the heat when we eat it later." He grinned, ducking out of her reach before she could swat him.

"You're lucky you're cute," she grumbled, slamming the cupboard closed again.

"Damn right, that's how I scored your fine little self." He winked, resting his hip against the counter. "Admit it, you love me."

With the hint of a smile on her face, she moped towards him, leaning her forehead into his chest. Damon's arms wrapped around her, pulling her close.

Sighing, she mumbled, "I *do* love you." And the truth was, she loved him more than she cared to admit. The thought of him fleeing when she dropped the baby bomb on him scared the crap out of her. Every time she went to do it, her voice would catch in her throat and she'd falter. It'd been a few days since she'd agreed to tell him, and she hadn't missed the disapproving looks Maddi had been firing her way.

Her shoulders shook as she fought the tears that were always so close to the surface.

"Hey." He cupped his hand under her chin, lifting gently. "Are you really this upset about a bowl of chilli?"

Biting her top lip, she closed her eyes. *It's now or never.*

"Damon, I—"

"Mmm, is that chilli I smell?" Maddi and Ricki strolled through the door, throwing their dance bags on the couch. "Smells divine."

Slipping out of Damon's arms, Rory swiped her tears away, coughing to clear her throat. "Ah, yeah. It's not ready yet. This big baby," she hooked a thumb over her shoulder, "thinks it's too spicy. I thought I might whip up a lime granita to serve with it."

"Ooh, that sounds delish." Maddi flopped down on the couch, kicking her feet up underneath her.

"Mmhmm, hopefully." Rory chewed her lip, avoiding Damon's eye as she pulled her blender out of the cupboard.

"Rory?" He stepped in behind her. "What were you going to say?"

"Hmm? Oh, um, never mind. I'll, um, tell you later." She waved her hand, shooing him from the kitchen while she went about gathering the ingredients she needed. Her heart was pounding in her chest, her fingers fumbling with the cord as she attempted to plug it in. Placing her hands on the bench, she lowered her head and closed her eyes, inhaling a deep breath through her nose and huffing it out her mouth. She would tell him tonight. Maybe.

Chapter 30

Ricki watched as Maddi went through her solo shine for what had to be the twentieth time. They'd had an extra training session with the team earlier on, and now it was just the two of them in the studio. She had always been a perfectionist when it came to her routines, and he knew she was adding extra pressure on herself with this performance being a dedication. But he was worried that she was overdoing it. He didn't really know a lot about having babies, but he was pretty sure that stress wasn't something she needed right now.

"Maddi, don't you think you should take a break? You've been at it for hours." He switched the music off, holding the remote firmly in his grasp.

"I've almost got it, just one more run through." She stood in front of the mirror, her arms positioned above her head. When he folded his arms across his chest and raised an eyebrow at her, she huffed out a breath, turning to face him. "What's the problem? You know how important this is."

Walking towards her, he gestured the length of her body. "Look at you, you're exhausted. It's okay to take a break, you know?"

She cocked her head, placing her hands on her hips. "Thanks for the vote of confidence," she said drily. "I'm fine. I just want to get this right. We've only got a few more weeks until the comps, and it needs to be perfect."

Tucking the remote into his back pocket, he ran his hands down her arms, taking her hands in his. "I know, and it will be." He kissed the tip of her nose. "It already is." His eyes dropped to her stomach and back up again. "I'm just trying to look after you. I don't want you overdoing it. You'll burn out."

"One more time, then I promise I'll stop and we can go back home, okay?"

Shaking his head with a chuckle, he held the remote over his shoulder, pressing play. "So damn stubborn."

Padding out of the bathroom in a comfy pair of trackies and a singlet, Maddi flopped onto the couch, tucking her legs beneath her. Pulling her hair over her shoulder, she dragged a brush through her mane.

"How was your bath? Feeling better?" Ricki asked as he settled in beside her with their hot chocolates.

"Mmm, it was just what I needed." She set her brush down, stretching her arms above her head with a satisfied sigh. "I didn't realise how tense I was."

"You really need to start looking after yourself, Maddi." He pursed his lips, deciding to just lay it all out there. "It's not just you you've got to think about now."

Turning to face him, she scrunched her nose. "What's that supposed to mean?"

In one fluid movement, he dropped to his knees in front of her. "I know." He waited a beat to gauge her reaction. "About the baby."

Her eyes widened as she chanced a glance in Rory's direction. "Ricki, I—"

He held his hand up to stop her. "It's okay, I understand why you didn't say anything. But I want you to know that I'm here for you and our baby. I won't let you go through this alone. We're a team, and a pretty good one, I think." He smiled, rummaging in his pocket for the box he'd been carrying around for the last few days, waiting for the right moment to present itself. "I messed everything up when I tried to go big and showy, so this time, I'm keeping it simple." With shaking hands, he held the tiny box out to her, opening the lid to reveal a rose-gold band with diamonds set in the shape of a flower on top. Maddi's hand flew to her chest, and her eyes welled. "Maddi, I love you more than anything. You're the most kind-hearted, beautiful soul I've ever met. You light up the room with just your smile, and when you dance… the whole world stops. I can't imagine my life without you in it, and I'm so excited to start our family together. Would you please do me the honour of being my wife?"

"Oh my God," she whispered. "I don't know what to say."

"Well, yes would be the preferred answer," Ricki joked with a nervous laugh.

"I have to tell you something, and I don't know if that will change things or not, but you need to know before I answer you." She looked at Rory, who had tears running down her face, whether from joy or fear, she wasn't sure.

"Okaaaay. You can tell me anything, you know that." He took her hand in his.

"Um, there's no easy way to say this. There's not… there's no baby. I'm not pregnant."

His face paled. "You…you lost the baby?" His words were barely audible. "Oh, Maddi, I'm so sorry. I can't believe you had to go through that on your own."

"No!" She shook her head, dropping to her knees to cradle his face. "That's not what I meant." She glanced over at Rory again. "I was never pregnant."

"But Damo saw you buy the test, and I found it in the trash. It was positive." He stared at her, confused.

"It was mine," Rory whispered, a sob catching in her throat. Turning to Damon, she broke down completely. "It was my positive test. I'm pregnant."

Chapter 31

"You're… You're… and we're… I'm going to be a father?" Damon stuttered, trying to wrap his head around what she was saying.

"Yes," she hiccupped, peering at him through her tears. "I'm s-so s-sorry I didn't tell y-you. We haven't t-talked about having children, and…" She took a deep breath to get the words out. "I was afraid you'd leave," she said quietly, lowering her head to stare at her fingers.

He tilted her chin up, wiping her tears from her cheeks. "Baby, look at me." With a trembling lip, she raised her eyes to meet his. "I'd have to be some kind of arsehole to get up and leave you because you're carrying my baby." He paused, pulling a face. "Wait, it *is* mine, right? I'm the baby daddy?"

"Of course you are!" she cried, punching his arm.

"Okay, okay!" He held his hands up in defence. "I was only joking. I know you've only got eyes for the D-man." He puffed his chest out. "Got you to stop crying though, didn't it?" His eyebrows waggled up and down, making her grin.

"I guess."

"Seriously though, why would I leave? You're drop-dead gorgeous and a phenomenal chef who will one day own her own café, earning us the big bucks, while I become a house-husband and look after the children. Sounds like a pretty sweet deal to me." He flexed his fingers, placing his hands behind his head as he stretched his legs out in front of him.

"You want to be a house-husband?" She quirked an eyebrow.

"Hell yeah! I'm not going to stand in the way of your dreams, and let's face it, I'm a big kid at heart, it makes sense for me to be the one who stays at home with them."

"So… we're doing this? Together?" She couldn't keep the hope from her voice.

"We're doing this. It would take a lot more than that to get rid of me."

With a squeal, she flung her arms around his neck, planting kisses all over his face.

"You keep that up and we'll be having twins!" He chuckled, wrapping his arms around her.

"I don't think that's how it works, Damo," Maddi said with a laugh. She knew in her heart he'd come through for her.

"Ah." Ricki cleared his throat. "I, um, don't want to take away from this heartfelt moment, but, um, you're kind of leaving me hanging here."

"Oh my God!" Maddi clamped her hands to her cheeks, turning to face him. "Sorry, I got caught up in the moment. Of course I'll marry you." She reached out to trace a finger along his jaw. "If you'll still have me, that is. I'm sorry there's no baby."

"Are you kidding? That just means we get to have fun trying." He winked, holding the ring up. "May I?"

"You better!" She giggled, extending her hand towards him so he could slide the ring on. "It's so beautiful," she gushed, staring at the glistening gems.

"Not nearly as beautiful as you."

Epilogue

"Good evening, ladies and gentlemen! And welcome to the National Salsa Championships!" The crowd erupted, hooting and hollering. "We have a fabulous group of performers lined up for you tonight, including a special tribute performance for one of our fallen stars. As many of you will know, the community was rocked only a month ago, by the death of one of our up-and-coming dancers, Sacha Barrett. Her presence will be sadly missed, and I ask you all to honour her with a moment's silence."

As everyone lowered their heads, the auditorium fell into silence. Backstage, Maddi grasped Jessie's hand, knowing how much this meant to him. She really hoped he liked the routine they'd put together in Sacha's memory. It would be the first time he'd seen it, and she was a little nervous.

"Thank you, everyone. Now, without further ado, let's get this show started! First up, we have the groups section!" A round of applause rang out as the groups gathered round behind the curtain. "Our first act comes all the way from Christchurch! Please welcome, the Southern Stars!"

"This is for you and Sacha," Maddi said, pecking Jessie on the cheek before taking Ricki's hand. Nicole and Rob were waiting in the wings on the other side of the stage, along with the rest of the team. Ricki took his place centre stage, with Maddi behind him. There was a hush over the crowd as the music began, and to the back of the stage, projections with images of Sacha lit up the darkness while Maddi did her slow walk around Ricki.

One by one, the other couples joined them on the stage, each weaving a tale with their bodies. When the song transitioned into their original piece, they picked up the pace, throwing their all into the routine. Behind them, the images continued to scroll through, showcasing Sacha's salsa journey, and of course, her relationship with Jessie.

When it was time for their solo shines, Maddi moved with fluidity across the stage, stopping in front of Ricki, with her back to the audience. Confused as to why she wasn't in the correct position, he raised his head to see if she was okay. What he saw, brought tears to his eyes. The other dancers faded into the background as she stood before him, holding her suit jacket open with a message sewn into the red satin:

You + Me = Three

Before he could respond, she'd spun away to join the rest of the girls for their ladies' shine. With the biggest grin on his face, he shook his head, falling into step with Rob.

The crowd went wild as the final beat was played and the dancers stepped forward to take their bows. Maddi clapped towards the side of the stage, beckoning Jessie to join them. He poked his head out from the curtain, giving a wave to the audience, before darting back again. He had tears in his eyes as he mouthed *Thank you* to her.

"Thank you, Southern Stars! What a fantastic performance! Give them one last round of applause before our next act comes to the stage!"

Jessie shook each of their hands as they made their way backstage. "Thanks, guys, that was amazing."

"You really liked it?" Maddi asked, ignoring his outstretched hand and pulling him in for a hug.

"It was perfect. She would have loved it."

"Maddi." Ricki tapped her on the shoulder. "Sorry, Jess, can I borrow her for a minute?"

Chuckling, Jessie unpeeled her arms from around him, handing her over. "By all means."

Taking her hand, he led her to one of the empty changing rooms. Closing the door behind him, he turned slowly. "Did that mean what I think it means?" he asked, searching her eyes.

A small smile graced her lips as she nodded. "Yeah, I think it does. It appears there *was* a baby after all."

"Really?"

"Really."

A knock on the door interrupted them, and Rory burst through the door. "Did you tell him yet?" She bounced up and down as Damon watched her with amusement.

"Sorry, guys, I tried to keep her out there as long as I could."

Maddi laughed. "It's okay, I told him already."

"We're gonna have twin bellies, and our kids will be the best of friends too!" She ran and tackle-hugged them both. "This is going to be so much fun!"

"Oh, I know!" Damon squealed and clapped his hands like an excited teenager before jumping in on the hug. He clamped a hand on Ricki's shoulder. "Congratulations, man."

"Thanks."

"Hey, what do you say we celebrate with a little drink?" He produced a bottle of sparkling grape juice from his pack, holding it in the air. "Non-alcoholic, of course." Popping the cork, he swiftly poured four cups, handing them out. "To shitty diapers and sleepless nights!"

They clinked their polystyrene cups together. Maddi glanced around at her best friends. It had been one hell of a year, and it was only going to get more interesting as their lives moved on to the next stage. Their destiny stretched out ahead of them, but if Maddi knew one thing, it was that they could make it through anything, as long as they had each other.

A note from the Author

Hello! Thank you for taking the time to read the final instalment to the A Step in Time series, with my novella "Dancing with Destiny". I hope you enjoyed reading it as much as I enjoyed writing it.

If you happened to enjoy my story, perhaps you could leave a brief review—reviews help authors' work to be seen, as well as providing us with feedback to improve.

Thanks again!

Stacey Broadbent

Other Books by Stacey Broadbent

Standalone

Never Judge a Book
Deep Heat

A Step in Time Series

Dancing Through the Storm
Dancing in Circles
Dancing with Destiny
A Step in Time: the complete series

Hollywood Novels

Emma

Flesh-Eater Series

Fear the Fever
Fight the Fever

Dark Sins Novellas

Sins of the Flesh
Mine

Ink-Slinging Sisters

Awesome Applesauce

Super Mum Series

Frazzled
Frazzled and Frumpy
Frazzled, Frumpy and Fabulous!
Super Mum: the complete series

Short stories and poetry

Musings, Mournings, and Misadventures

Anthologies

The White Ribbon Collection
Scars to your Beautiful
Witching Hour: Vices and Virtues
Key to my Heart
A Touch of Inspiration
No Place like Home
Serendipity

Acknowledgements

It's a little bittersweet that I write these final words of acknowledgement, ending the Dancing novella series. These characters were the first ones I ever wrote about, and so they hold a special place in my heart. It means the world to me that you, the reader, have followed me on this journey. Without you, none of this would be possible.

I also have to give thanks to my support crew, Shannon and the Ink Slinging Sisters! You guys are my cheerleaders when I need picking up, and I adore each and every one of you!

The person who has been with me from the beginning, encouraging me to put pen to paper; Trina. Your friendship and eagle eye mean so much to me. I really don't think I could do this without you.

Special thanks go out to the salsa community for being my stress release over the years. I made some great friends, and had a lot of fun with you all. Keep on dancing!

And last, but not least, to my family. Thank you for allowing me to follow my dreams. I love you all xxx

Connect with me

http://www.staceybroadbent.weebly.com

https://www.facebook.com/StaceyBroadbentAuthor

Broadbent's Bookish Babes: https://goo.gl/FY9wQN

https://www.amazon.com/author/staceybroadbent

Goodreads: https://goo.gl/YJ6dXa

https://www.instagram.com/authorstaceybroadbent/

https://www.bookbub.com/authors/stacey-broadbent

https://vm.tiktok.com/ZSJBb5bhL/

Sign up for my newsletter:
http://eepurl.com/cULu_f

About the Author

Stacey resides in Ashburton, New Zealand with her husband and three children. She is a qualified proofreader, author, wife, mother, and self-proclaimed culinary goddess. When she's not busy writing or editing books, she enjoys reading and procrastinating on TikTok.

She absolutely loves hearing from readers, so please feel free to reach out via email, Instagram, or join her reader group, Broadbent's Bookish Babes. You can also sign up to her newsletter for up-to-date info on releases.